I had seen his old Buick parked in front of Higher Grounds when I acted like I had no idea he had a car and offered him a ride.

"Isn't she still married to Cephus Hardy?" My eyes zeroed in on his facial expression.

Cephus jumped around me and grabbed Terk by the neck. "Yeah, you sonofabitch!"

"Stop!" I yelled, but it was too late. Terk was feeling the effect of Cephus's revenge.

Terk choked out a lung, bent over, and continued to hack.

"Need. A. Beer," he gasped, holding one hand up to his throat and the other pointed into the trailer.

I rushed past him and made a sharp right turn into the kitchen, where there was a round café table, two chairs, a small counter with a sink, and a few upper cabinets that had yellowed from the cigarette smoke.

There was a piece of paper lying on the table with Cephus Hardy printed big and bold at the top. Without even looking at it and without thinking, I grabbed it and stuck it in my pocket.

By Tonya Kappes

TONYA KAPPES

A

GHOSTLY DEMISE

A GHOSTLY SOUTHERN MYSTERY

WITNESS

An Imprint of HarperCollinsPublishers

This is a work of fiction. Names, characters, places, and incidents are products of the author's imagination or are used fictitiously and are not to be construed as real. Any resemblance to actual events, locales, organizations, or persons, living or dead, is entirely coincidental.

WITNESS

An Imprint of HarperCollins*Publishers*
195 Broadway
New York, New York 10007

Copyright © 2015 by Tonya Kappes
Excerpt from *A Ghostly Murder* copyright © 2015 by Tonya Kappes
ISBN 978-0-06-237491-2
www.witnessimpulse.com

First Witness mass market printing: September 2015

HarperCollins ® is a registered trademark of HarperCollins Publishers.

Printed in the United States of America

10 9 8 7 6 5 4 3 2 1

A
GHOSTLY
DEMISE

Chapter 1

"Cephus Hardy?"

Stunned. My jaw dropped when I saw Cephus Hardy walk up to me in the magazine aisle of Artie's Meat and Deli. I was admiring the cover of *Cock and Feathers*, where my last client at Eternal Slumber Funeral Home, Chicken Teater, graced the cover with his prize Orloff Hen, Lady Cluckington.

"I declare." A Mack truck could've hit me and I wouldn't have felt it. I grinned from ear to ear.

Cephus Hardy looked the exact same as he did five years ago. Well, from what I could remember from his social visits with my momma and daddy and the few times I had seen him around our small town of Sleepy Hollow, Kentucky.

His tight, light brown curls resembled a baseball helmet. When I was younger, it amazed me how thick and dense his hair was. He always wore polyester taupe pants with the perfectly straight crease down the front, along with a brown belt. The hem of his pants ended right above the shoelaces in his white, patent-leather shoes. He tucked in his short-sleeved, plaid shirt, making it so taut you could see his belly button.

"Momma and Daddy live in Florida now, but they are going to be so happy when I tell them you are back in town. Everyone has been so worried about you." I smiled and took in his sharp, pointy nose and rosy red cheeks. I didn't take my eyes off him as I put the copy of *Cock and Feathers* back in the rack. I leaned on my full cart of groceries and noticed he hadn't even aged a bit. No wrinkles. Nothing. "Where the hell have you been?"

He shrugged. He rubbed the back of his neck.

"Who cares?" I really couldn't believe it. Mary Anna was going to be so happy since he had just up and left five years ago, telling no one—nor had he contacted anyone since. "You won't believe what Granny is doing."

I pointed over his shoulder at the election

poster taped up on Artie's Meat and Deli's store-front window.

"Granny is running against O'Dell Burns for mayor." I cackled, looking in the distance at the poster of Zula Fae Raines Payne all laid-back in the rocking chair on the front porch of the Sleepy Hollow Inn with a glass of her famous iced tea in her hand.

It took us ten times to get a picture she said was good enough to use on all her promotional items for the campaign. Since she was all of five-foot-four, her feet dangled. She didn't want people to vote on her size; therefore, the photo was from the lap up. I told Granny that I didn't know who she thought she was fooling. Everyone who was eligible to vote knew her and how tall she was. She insisted. I didn't argue anymore. No one, and I mean no one, wins an argument against Zula Fae Raines Payne. Including me.

"She looks good." Cephus raised his brows, lips turned down.

"She sure does," I noted.

For a twice-widowed seventy-seven-year-old, Granny acted like she was in her fifties. I wasn't sure if her red hair was still hers or if Mary Anna kept it up on the down-low, but Granny would never be seen going to Girl's Best Friend unless there was some sort of gossip that needed to be heard. Otherwise, she wanted everyone to see her as the good Southern belle she was.

"Against O'Dell Burns?" Cephus asked. Slowly, he nodded in approval.

It was no secret that Granny and O'Dell had butted heads a time or two. The outcome of the election was going to be interesting, to say the least.

"Yep. She retired three years ago, leaving me and Charlotte Rae in charge of Eternal Slumber."

It was true. I was the undertaker of Eternal Slumber Funeral Home. It might make some folks' skin crawl to think about being around dead people all the time, but it was job security at its finest. O'Dell Burns owned Burns Funeral, the other funeral home in Sleepy Hollow, which made him and Granny enemies from the get-go.

O'Dell didn't bother me though. Granny didn't see it that way. We needed a new mayor, and O'Dell stepped up to the plate at the council meeting, but Granny wouldn't hear of it. So the competition didn't stop with dead people; now Granny wants all the living people too. As mayor.

"Long story short," I rambled on and on, "Granny married Earl Way Payne. He died and left Granny the Sleepy Hollow Inn. I don't know what she is thinking running for mayor because she's so busy taking care of all of the tourists at the Inn. Which reminds me"—I planted my hands on my hips—"you never answered my question. Have you seen Mary Anna yet?"

"Not yet." His lips curved in a smile.

"She's done real good for herself. She opened Girl's Best Friend Spa and has all the business since she's the only one in town. And"—I wiggled my brows—"she is working for me at Eternal Slumber."

A shiver crawled up my spine and I did a little shimmy shake, thinking about her fixing the corpses' hair and makeup. Somebody had to do it and Mary Anna didn't seem to mind a bit.

I ran my hand down my brown hair that Mary Anna had recently dyed since my short stint as a blond. I couldn't do my own hair, much less someone else's. Same for the makeup department.

I never spent much time in front of the mirror. I worked with the dead and they weren't judging me.

"Emma Lee?" Doc Clyde stood at the end of the magazine aisle with a small shopping basket in the crook of his arm. His lips set in a tight line. "Are you feeling all right?"

"Better than ever." My voice rose when I pointed

to Cephus. "Especially now that Cephus is back in town."

"Have you been taking your meds for the Funeral Trauma?" He ran his free hand in his thin hair, placing the few remaining strands to the side. His chin was pointy and jutted out even more as he shuffled his thick-soled doctor shoes down the old, tiled floor. "You know, it's only been nine months since your accident. And it could take years before the symptoms go away."

"Funeral Trauma," I muttered, and rolled my eyes.

Cephus just grinned.

The Funeral Trauma.

A few months back I had a perilous incident with a plastic Santa Claus right here at Artie's Meat and Deli. I had walked down from the funeral home to grab some lunch. Artie had thought it was a good idea to put a life-sized plastic Santa on the roof. It was a good idea until the snow started melting and the damn thing slid right off the roof just as I was walking by, knocking me square out. Flat.

I woke up in the hospital seeing ghosts of the corpses I had buried six feet deep. I thought I had gone to the Great Beyond. But I could see my family and all the living.

I told Doc Clyde I was having some sort of hallucinations and seeing dead people. He said I had been in the funeral business a little too long and seeing corpses all of my life had been traumatizing. Granny had been in the business for over forty years. I had only been in the business for three. Something didn't add up.

Turned out, a psychic confirmed I am what was called a Betweener.

I could see ghosts of the dead who were stuck between the here and the after. Of course, no one but me and Jack Henry, my boyfriend and Sleepy Hollow's sheriff, knew. And he was still a little apprehensive about the whole thing.

"I'm fine," I assured Doc Clyde, and looked at Cephus. "Wait." I stopped and tried to swallow what felt like a mound of sand in my mouth. My mind hit rewind and took me back to the beginning of my conversation with Cephus.

Chapter 2

"Outta the way!" I pushed past Doc Clyde, leaving the cartful of groceries, and made it to the front of the store. "Outta the way!" I yelled at Beulah Paige Bellefry.

"I *dee*-clare." Beulah grabbed the pearls around her neck like I was going to do a drive-by robbery. I pushed my way past her. "I'm calling Zula Fae!"

I stopped dead in my tracks and stood on the sidewalk in front of the hearse. Slowly, I turned around.

The bag boy and clerk had their faces planted up against the glass next to Granny's election poster while Doc Clyde and Beulah stood with their hands on their hips, taking in all my crazy. Beulah Paige's ice-blue eyes cut right through me.

She batted her fake lashes, tucked a strand of her flaming red hair behind her ear and whispered something to Doc Clyde.

"I'm sure you will tell everyone in Sleepy Hollow," I shouted back at the window—confirming Beulah Paige's reign as the CEO of the gossip mill in the small town.

I jumped in the hearse.

It took everything in my body not to ram my hearse into her red Cadillac, which was parked in front of me.

"I'm sorry, Emma Lee." Cephus appeared in the passenger seat next to me.

My jaw clenched, my hands gripped the wheel so hard my knuckles were white. I couldn't bring myself to look at him. Not for the fact that he scared me, but rather because it meant he was dead. Dead as dead could be. How was I going to explain that to Mary Anna and her brother?

"I'm just so glad, after all these years, to have some help."

"Years?" I asked.

Had he been dead this entire time? The rumor was that he had gone on a binge and left his family behind.

He nodded. "The *entire* time."

"Who says I'm going to help you?" I asked.

Deep down I knew I was going to have to. I was hooked from the moment I realized he was a ghost. I slammed the brakes on the hearse and looked over at him.

"Seriously, years?" I asked again, just to make sure.

"I didn't leave town like everyone thinks." His eyes took on a ghostly look. He turned his face toward the window. "I was murdered and I can't cross over to live in peace."

"That loudmouth Ruthie Sue Payne," I growled.

"Ruthie Sue." Cephus shook his head and smiled.

Ruthie Sue was the town gossip before she died . . . was murdered. She was my first client as a Betweener. After I helped solve her murder, I found out she was a big gossip in the afterlife too. She told Chicken Teater about me, who was my second client. Now Chicken had told Cephus . . . who I had no choice but to help.

"You know I have to help." I pushed the gas, headed down Main Street and out of town to the police station. "Or you will haunt me the rest of my life."

"I sure do appreciate it though I could use an ice-cold Stroh's." Only it sounded like "Stro." He smacked his lips together.

"Stroh's?" I asked, putting the "h" in.

I wondered if they still made the bitter beer.

"Yeah, ice-cold Stroh's." He left the "h" off again. He twisted his body around and looked in the back of the hearse. "You could put a big beer cooler back there."

"No, I don't have an ice-cold Stroh's," I said with an emphasis the "h."

"Where are we going?" he asked. "To the Watering Hole?" He rubbed his hands together in excitement.

"No." My eyes narrowed, wondering if my ghostly Cephus Hardy had a slight drinking problem. "We are going to see Jack Henry."

"Why?" His face contorted. "I don't care about no ball game. I'd much rather go visit the boys at the bar."

"We aren't going to the ball game." I pointed ahead to the SLEEPY HOLLOW POLICE DEPARTMENT sign. "You have to remember, you've been dea . . ." I stopped myself, " . . . gone for five years. There isn't even a men's softball league anymore."

"No beer-drinking night?" Cephus asked in a whiny voice.

All the men in Sleepy Hollow used to play "softball" at the old field as a cover-up for beer-drinking night. Jack Henry Ross included.

"Are you telling me Jack Henry is in charge of Sleepy Hollow?"

"That's exactly what I'm telling you. And if you are here, that means he has probably found your body or knows something." I turned into the station lot and was happy to see his sheriff's car there.

"Give me all the deets." I walked in the small, crackerbox station.

Jack Henry Ross was reclined back in his chair, Lexington newspaper in hand and feet propped up on top of his desk. He smiled. His big brown eyes caused my heart to skip. All he had to do was look at me with those eyes and I melted. If he ever broke up with me, I'd probably be joining Cephus.

Granny always said that a broken heart was like trying to freeze broken chocolate, no matter how hard you try, you'll never return it to its original shape.

"Hey there." He stood up to greet me. Mary Anna must've just cut his hair because it was high and tight like he loved it. "I was just wondering what you had gotten from Artie's for our romantic dinner tonight."

"Groceries." I groaned. "Damn. I left them in the middle of the magazine aisle with Doc Clyde."

"Damn." Cephus got close to Jack and tilted his

head to get a good look. He put his hand on his neck and rubbed. "He ain't squirrelly anymore. He's got some muscles."

"Tell me where you found him." I ignored Cephus and walked over, curled up on my toes and gave him a sweet hello kiss. That was all he was getting until I got my information. "I didn't drive all the way out here to get schmoozed. I know you don't like it when I'm involved, but I can't help it if they come to me."

"Who came to you?" He pulled back. His loving brown eyes turned to curiosity.

Cephus squatted and took a good long look at Jack's gun. "Damn. They have some good stuff."

"Funny." My eyes lowered. The phone in my back pocket buzzed. I pulled it out. Granny was calling and I knew exactly why. Doc Clyde or Beulah Paige had gotten ahold of her. I ignored it and put it back in my pocket. "You are pulling my leg."

"No, Emma Lee." He shook his head. "Nothing has come in. It's dead silent around here. The way I like it."

The phone buzzed again.

"Aren't you going to get that? It must be important." Jack gestured toward my pocket.

"Granny," I said with a little sarcasm. Not that

Granny wasn't important; I wasn't in a mood to hear her say that I needed some Funeral Trauma medication, nor did I have an excuse figured out to explain my peculiar behavior in the middle of the magazine aisle.

"It's not going to be silent for long." I sucked in a deep breath. I pointed to Cephus Hardy, who was taking way too much interest in Jack's gun. "Jack Henry Ross, meet Cephus Hardy."

Cephus stood up and put his hand out like Jack could see him.

"He can't see you and he has never been squirrelly." I made sure I took up for Jack Henry.

It wasn't long ago when Jack Henry and I had become an item, a hot and heavy item. Well, not so hot, but still. We were dating after years—and I mean years—of me lusting after him. Little did I know, until recently, that he had felt the same about me all those years ago.

Tonight, we were having dinner at my place to help make up for lost time.

"Squirrelly?" Jack Henry's mouth dropped. That got his attention. "He called me squirrelly?"

"Never mind him." I waved off the comment. "He's dead. Not missing. Dead."

"Boo!" Cephus giggled and jumped around, trying to scare Jack Henry.

"For the last time, he can't see you," I said with exhaustion.

Cephus was wearing my patience thin.

Clearly, Cephus wasn't good at this ghost thing and I was going to have to lay down some ground rules.

Just then, the Sleepy Hollow police station phone rang. Jack Henry said a few yeps, okays, and fines before he hung up the phone.

"I've gotta go. Somebody let Sanford Brumfield's goats out and they are eating up all of Dottie Kramer's vegetables." He grabbed his keys and popped his hat back on his head, making me lose all my senses. "Go back and grab the groceries and we can talk about this situation," he said, and twirled his finger around.

"When we go back, can you pick me up a pack of cold Stroh's?" Cephus asked, and stood between me and my man.

"Enough of the Stroh's!" I shouted to the air between me and Jack Henry.

Jack Henry snapped his finger.

"That's what Teddy used to say about his dad at practice." Jack Henry said in his slow, Southern drawl. He pretended to mock Teddy, Cephus's son, "Son, get me an ice-cold Stroh's."

Jack Henry left off the "h" exactly like Cephus did.

"That little shit made fun of me?" Cephus asked Jack Henry.

"Last time." I shook my finger at Cephus Hardy. "He. Can. Not. Hear. You."

"Good luck with the goats. I'll see you tonight." I walked out the door with Jack Henry.

"Where is he?" Jack Henry put his hand on my arm.

"Who?" I asked.

"Cephus Hardy."

"Right here." I pointed beside me.

"No, not the ghost." Jack Henry shook his head. "The body."

"Oh. I don't know." I turned to Cephus. "Where's your body?"

"That I do not know. But a cold Stroh's might help me remember." Cephus smiled from ear to ear.

"Looks like this one is going to be harder than the last two." I bit my lip and took a deep breath before I gave Jack Henry the bad news. "He doesn't know where his body is."

My first Betweener client, Ruthie Sue, was a fresh body. And Chicken Teater was a little harder than Ruthie because we had to exhume his body.

With both of them, we were able to have the body to examine for clues to determine that they were in fact murdered. Here, I was going on a ghost's word that he was murdered, making it much harder for Jack Henry to investigate.

"Houston"—Jack Henry made a megaphone with his hands and called out into the air—"we have a problem."

Chapter 3

et me tell you how this works. I will do the sleuthing. You give me any details. Other than that, I can't have you talking to the living." I kept my eyes peeled for anyone looking at me. "And don't interrupt me when I'm talking to the living. I can't concentrate on you and them at the same time. It screws my head up."

"I've never been much of a rule follower," Cephus warned.

"Maybe that is a reason you were murdered," I quipped.

Cephus harrumphed and folded his arms.

"I didn't know Teddy was on the baseball team." I made small talk. Maybe it made him feel good to talk about his kids. Especially his son. "I knew he did something with fighting or something."

"Wrastlin'," Cephus said proudly, rolling his shoulders forward.

"Wrastlin'?" I asked. "Is that some sort of country sport?"

Cephus Hardy and his family lived in the holler on the outskirts of town. Mary Anna and her brother used to have the best parties, or so I heard. I wasn't the most popular girl in school.

Jack Henry Ross was an athlete, putting him at the top of the popular list. Me . . . not so much. No one wanted to hang around the creepy, funeral-home girl. But look at me now. I had Jack Henry and a successful business. Not like the popular girls who were barefoot and pregnant, living in the trailer park next to the cemetery.

"Wrastlin'!" Cephus did some sort of moves with his hands.

"Wrestling," I confirmed. "That's right. I remember now. He was pretty good at that, wasn't he?"

I vaguely recalled something about it, but Teddy was younger than me.

"Made it to the state championship." Cephus's eyes lit up as he told me about all the matches and medals Teddy had won.

"Gosh, I wonder where Teddy is now?" I

couldn't even tell Cephus what his son was doing. As far as I could remember, he left after high school and never come back. "Mary Anna in passing did say that your leaving town affected Teddy the most."

"I didn't leave town." Cephus jerked back. "I'm telling you, someone killed me." He rubbed the back of his neck.

"Who did it?" I asked. "If you tell me, then we can solve this thing easy."

It made perfect sense to me. He tells me who the murderer was, I tell Jack Henry, Jack Henry arrested them, Cephus crosses over, and Jack Henry and I have our date.

"I don't know. I told you that," he said loudly.

"Not where your body is." His body would not be in good condition after five years. "Who did it."

"I do not know." His brows furrowed in frustration. "Hey, Sleepy Hollow sure does look good."

Cephus stared out the passenger window. Even in the last years, Sleepy Hollow had made some big changes.

"The town council offered a lot of incentives to help bring business to the area. Over the past few years, the economy has taken a boost from the caves being open." I gestured toward the mountainous backdrop of our little town. "You wouldn't believe how many tourists we get who want to explore the caves. In fact, there are so many tours there now. And Sanford Brumfield is one of the tour guides."

"Is that right?" The look on Cephus's face made my heart ache. His eyes darted back and forth across Main Street so I made sure I drove slow. He was taking it all in.

"Mmmhmm." I left it at that.

Main Street had really been cleaned up by the Beautification Committee over the past few years and looked somewhat different from five years ago.

They put in a new streetscape with gas lanterns and hooks for hanging plants. There was even a spot on them for banners with the Sleepy Hollow logo, which was a backdrop of the mountains and caves.

I couldn't imagine how hard it would be to be stuck between worlds and come back to your home and find out everything had changed.

"What's that?"

"Higher Grounds Café. A coffee shop." I sure could use a jolt of coffee from there. "Do you remember the Doyles? Mary Anna's friend, Cheryl Lynne Doyle?"

"Naw." He shook his head. Not a hair on his head even moved.

"Anyway, Cheryl Lynne owns the coffee shop," I said.

Something in the rearview mirror caught my eye. A white flag was waving in the wind. I pushed the hearse's gas pedal when I saw that it was Granny whizzing out of the parking lot of the Sleepy Hollow Inn.

I hadn't answered her call and I was positive Doc Clyde or Beulah had gotten to her. Instead of driving on the street, she took a shortcut across the town square, not paying a bit of attention to anyone who might be in her way. Including the traveling carnival that was in town.

The carnival was a small affair that went from small town to small town all over the state. It came in on a few buses, along with a few games like the water-balloon game and the dunk tank, carnival rides like the tilt-a-whirl, and pitched a tent right in the middle of towns. Luckily, the square was a great spot for them.

The town square was a piece of land in the middle of the town, with four of the main streets of Sleepy Hollow going around it. It was where all the fun festivities were held. There was a gazebo in the middle of the nice park. On beautiful days like today, many people enjoyed their lunch in the square or rested in the sun. But this weekend, the carnival took up the space.

Beep, beep. A small horn came from the square.

"Move it!" Granny screamed.

She tried to steady the wobbly moped with one hand and used the other to wave people out of her way, using her sweet Southern charm.

She yelled over the buzz of the scooter motor, "Vote for Zula Fae for mayor." She pumped her fist in the air. "I appreciate your support."

Granny left no opportunity untaken.

Her moped was getting closer and I pushed the gas more. She looked between me and the funeral home, gauging her distance to determine how fast she needed to go to make sure we made it there at the same time.

"She went to college in New York City and all of these fancy coffee shops were there. She decided to open one . . . with her daddy's money," I added.

I zipped around the square into Eternal Slumber's parking lot, trying to beat Granny's shortcut.

I jumped out as fast as I could. The whiz of Granny and her moped were getting closer. Fast wasn't good enough. Granny was on a mission. Me.

I didn't even make it to the top step of the front porch of the funeral home before I heard her yelling my name.

"Emma Lee," Granny screamed over the buzz of her moped. "Emma Lee! I know you aren't ignoring me!"

I stopped, took a deep breath and closed my eyes before I turned toward her screeching. She wasn't going to give up until I answered her.

Mentally, I prepared myself for the tongue-lashing she was about to give me.

"Didn't you hear me way back there?" She came to a sliding stop. The flag on the back of her moped waved in the slight breeze.

One side had a big picture of Granny on it, the other side was printed with ZULA FAE FOR MAYOR! It was her best advertisement yet.

"Yes, I heard you."

"Then why didn't you stop?" Granny's eyes were magnified under her black-leather motorcycle touring half helmet and aviator goggles. Wisps of red hair stuck out from underneath her tight leather helmet.

"I have to go to work." I poked my keys toward the front door of the funeral home.

"Dang"—Cephus stood next to Granny—"Zula Fae is looking better than ever."

Ahem. I cleared my throat in hopes Cephus would shut up like I had asked him to earlier.

"You will do no such thing," Granny warned. "You will take you and your crazy right over to Doc Clyde's to get checked out, then go back to bed."

"I'm not crazy or tired."

Granny steadied the moped by planting her new black-leather-motorcycle-booted feet on each side.

Over her shoulder, I could see Doc Clyde giving us the eyeball from the gazebo in the middle of the square. That's when I knew.

"I see." I swallowed. "Doc Clyde has used my little hiccup as an excuse to come pay you a little social call."

Granny straightened her shoulders and put her chin in the air. "Emma Lee," she gasped, "I might be old, but I'm a good Southern woman. And what you did inside and outside at Artie's, I might add, was not a little hiccup."

"Oh, hodgepodge." My lips puckered. "I was teasing Doc Clyde when he was giving me the eye. You know I knew he was trying to assess me."

After a few more minutes of looking me over and lecturing me about how serious Funeral Trauma was, she seemed to realize I wasn't going to give in.

"Then come over to Higher Grounds and get a cup of coffee with me."

I gave her my best narrow-eyed look. "Then you will believe me?"

I could definitely use a cup of coffee.

She crossed her heart, kissed her finger, and held it up in the air to the Great Beyond.

"I'm not riding on that." I pointed to the moped.

In a flash, Granny whipped out a steel chain from the saddlebag attached to the side of her moped and some ZULA FOR MAYOR buttons. She chained the moped up to the tree in the front yard of Eternal Slumber.

Chapter 4

Higher Grounds Café was located on the front side of the square near the courthouse and several other small shops. Eternal Slumber was on the side of the square near Pose and Relax yoga studio.

It was a beautiful morning to take a stroll. The sun was already out and had burned off the morning fog that was always nestled in the mountainous backdrop. The smell of fresh air was good for the soul and the mind. I definitely needed some fresh air for my head.

Cephus had it all jumbled up. Questions kept darting in and I needed the mental power to process the questions. So a cup of coffee was definitely welcome, to burn away my brain fog.

"Wait. I don't want a coffee. I want an ice-cold Stroh's!" Cephus shouted from behind me and Granny as we crossed over Main Street toward Higher Grounds. "You have to get me to the other side. Chitchatting with Zula Fae isn't going to get me there."

Granny rambled on about her campaign and how she wanted John Howard to stick a sign in the front yard of the funeral home.

"Sure," I agreed to keep the peace.

Having her talk about the campaign kept her from talking about my little episode this morning at Artie's. Plus, there was no harm in sticking a small yard sign in the front. O'Dell had one in the lawn of Burns Funeral Home. As Granny saw it, tit for tat.

"I'll be a sonofabitch." Cephus rushed ahead of us, catching my attention.

There was a beat-up, pale blue Buick parked in front of Higher Grounds Café that I didn't recognize. He did. He eased around the old junker, looking in all the windows.

"Where the hell is he?" he demanded to know. He marched up and down the street in front of the café, looking for whoever *he* was. "Where the hell is she?"

My eyes grew big. I swallowed hard. I had no

idea whom he was talking about and I couldn't ask him. At least not right this minute, with Granny sticking to my side like glue. And people walking around.

"Looks like something's going on in there." Granny pushed her way through the door into the crowd.

Some of the Auxiliary women—Mable Claire, Beulah Paige, and Hettie Bell—were standing in a circle around one of the small café tables. I couldn't see who was sitting down. Who were they talking to?

"Good morning!" Cheryl Lynne hollered above the crowd. "Two?" She made an air cup with her hand and put it to her lips.

I nodded. "I like the new shirts."

I couldn't help but notice the tight brown T-shirt with the yellow coffee cup, strategically placed right on top of her very endowed chest and showing off her perfect size-six frame. Her long blond hair lay perfectly over her shoulders.

"Thank you." The words oozed out of her red lips in the slow Southern drawl that drew men in like a bar did a drunk.

"Vote for Zula Fae Raines Payne." Granny handed a button to Dottie Kramer, who was dropping off her fresh carrots to Cheryl Lynne. "You let me take care of your loved ones, let me take care of you." Granny winked.

Sometimes a wink spoke louder than words. This was the case with Granny.

Cheryl Lynne used the carrots to make the best homemade carrot bran muffins.

"No thank you. I'm a Burns voter." Dottie Kramer pushed back Granny's hand and gave Granny a big, long, theatrical wink.

Dottie didn't bother getting dressed for her public appearances. She always seemed to wear the same thing. Housecoat, hairnet and white nurse's shoes.

"I dee-clare." Granny drew her hand to her chest and huffed on over to the crowded table. I followed behind, but not without staring down Dottie Kramer.

I averted my evil glance to Beulah Paige to let her know that she better not mention the little episode this morning.

Ahem. Beulah Paige cleared her throat and skittered out of the way, making room for me and Granny to see what all of the hubbub was about.

There sat a woman with frizzy hair pulled up in a topknot right on the top of her head. She gave a great big lopsided smile when she saw Granny. Her front tooth was missing. Next to the woman was Leotta Hardy, Cephus's widow. Someone I hadn't seen in quite a long time.

Granny gave Leotta a polite nod, as did I. But not Cephus.

"Ah'm fixin' ta kick some ass!" he warned.

He crouched with his arms to his side and swayed back and forth like he was ready for a throw-down.

"Zula Fae Raines." The frizzy-headed woman stood up and put her arms out to greet Granny. Her six-foot frame towered over little five-foot-four Granny, but that didn't stop her from giving out a big bear hug. "I mean Payne. Or whatever it is nowadays." She pulled back, giving Granny a wink. I wasn't sure, but I think she gave Granny a subtle dig. Granny took it in stride with a little laugh.

"How the hell are ya?" The woman gave Granny a pat on the back, only it was a little harder than a normal pat.

"I reckon I'm doing just fine." Granny never did say much beyond that. She considered it bragging. "How are you, Bea Allen?"

"Finer than frog hair." She pushed back a chair and patted it. "Sit down." Bea Allen gave a little toodles to Beulah Paige and her gang, sending them away and sitting back down in her chair.

"I'll catch up with you girls later." She turned her attention to Granny by crossing her legs. Her long dress rose up a little, exposing her feet.

Not the prettiest of sights. In fact, I had to turn away as her big toe was popped right out of the front of her sandals. Not a good look for Bea Allen, whoever she was.

"This here must be Emma Lee." She patted the other seat. "I hear you have been creating a lot of stir around here lately."

Not sure what to say, I eased into the chair and sat between her and Granny.

"But don't you worry about old Beulah Paige Bellefry. She's always thought she was hotter than Satan's housecoat." Bea Allen patted my knee before she turned her attention toward Granny. "What is this I hear about you running for mayor against my brother?"

Brother? I had always heard stories about Bea Allen Burns but had never personally gotten to meet her. She'd been long gone from Sleepy Hollow before I had even cared who lived there. I was a kid when she left. It wasn't like I kept up on the town gossip. Though when you lived in the funeral home, you learned that at a funeral, the vestibule was the best spot to be to find out anything you wanted to know about what was going

on in the town. As kids, many times Charlotte Rae
and I hid behind the thick, red-velvet drapes just
so we could get a glimpse of the Auxiliary women
in their fancy hats and clothes.

Funerals were a social gathering around these
parts and everyone always looked their finest.
Since Charlotte Rae and I didn't have many
friends, we had to play by ourselves and we
would reenact the conversations we would overhear. Granny or Momma would always tell us to
hush up and mind our own business. Spreading
idle gossip wasn't pretty and wasn't nice.

Pretty is as pretty does, Granny used to say.

Still, Charlotte always got to play Beulah Paige's
part because Beulah always dressed to the hilt
and never left home without her pearls. Me . . . I
was Mable Claire.

"It was good seeing you." Mable Claire softly
spoke over Granny's shoulder. She had her hair
pulled into a bun on the top of her head. Her
mouth turned into a full smile, causing the balls
on her cheeks to rise and her eyes to squint.
"Leotta, I'll call you later."

Leotta nodded. Still silent.

Beulah tugged at Mable Claire's arm, sending
Mable Claire's fuller hips into a giddyup. She jingled her way through the crowd stopping at each

child, pulling a dime from her pocket and handing them one as she patted them on the head.

Mable Claire was kind and thoughtful. She had always been nice to me. Beulah Paige on the other hand wasn't. Bea Allen was right. Beulah thought she was better than everyone.

"I knew! I knew it! I knew it!" Cephus had one hand on his hip while the other was in a tight fist, shaking it right at Leotta. "You little slut! I know that is Terk Rhinehammer's old Buick! I'd know it from a mile away."

Bea Allen and Granny made conversation, unaware of Cephus making a ruckus between them as Leotta kept to herself with her hands neatly folded in her lap. I bit my lip trying not to laugh as he carried on about how Terk had an eye for Leotta since high school. He even claimed Terk couldn't wait for him to die so he could slip into Leotta's life.

I grabbed my phone from my back pocket. If what Cephus said was true about Terk, maybe Terk had killed Cephus. This could be my first clue. I had learned that no stone can be unturned when you're trying to get the dead to do just that . . . die.

"Honey, have you heard from Cephus?" Granny turned her attention to Leotta.

Everyone went silent. Inwardly, I groaned. Leave it to Granny to ask such questions.

Since Leotta was Mary Anna's momma, Mary Anna wasn't going to let her mom go around town with gray roots. Leotta's hair was black as coal, along with her eyes. She reminded me of a younger version of Loretta Lynn, with her pointy nose, small mouth and thin chin. She wore a pair of capri jeans and a V-neck T-shirt that showed the top of cleavage. Just enough for men to take a look and use their imagination for what was under.

"Put on some clothes." Cephus stomped around the back of Leotta's chair.

It was the biggest uproar when Cephus didn't come home after a long weekend. Most people would worry if one of their loved ones didn't come home after one night, but Cephus Hardy was a different story.

He was known as the town drunk. He'd show up at the Watering Hole on Friday and not leave until Sunday morning, when there was no alcohol to be had. In Kentucky, the law stated that there were no alcohol sales on Sunday, which meant there were no bars open.

When he never made it home, Leotta knew something was wrong. I recalled Mary Anna telling Charlotte Rae about how Cephus would be in a stumbling, drunken stupor and her momma, Leotta, would spend most of Sunday sobering him up so he could go to work on Monday to earn his paycheck for next weekend's binge.

"No." Leotta gave a slight grin, exposing some pretty teeth. "Teddy has looked high and low for him. Best we figured, he must've traveled east like he always wanted to and found a bar on the beach. Never to come back. Nothing is certain."

"Honey"—Granny patted Leotta's hand—"nothing is certain except for death and taxes. He'll be back."

"Why would I come home when you are shacking up with Terk Rhinehammer!" Cephus jumped up in the air like he was doing some sort of wrestling move. "I'll put him in a sleeper hold."

"Terk Rhinehammer?" I asked out loud, and quickly shut my mouth.

Damn, damn, damn. I closed my eyes, hoping no one heard me.

"Did you say Terk?" Leotta leaned around Bea Allen to put her cold, coal-black eyes on me.

"What?" Granny pulled back and glared at me. "What's Terk got to do with Cephus Hardy?"

"Nothing." I shook my head and put two and two together. The car that Cephus was up in arms about had to be Terk's. "Isn't that Terk Rhinehammer's car out there?" I pointed to the street.

"How would you know that is his car?" Leotta's eyes lowered.

"He used to drive that over to see Daddy," I lied. As far as I knew, Daddy didn't even know Terk, but Leotta didn't know that.

"Good one." Cephus pursed his lips and nodded, never once taking his eyes off Leotta. "Terk would never go see your daddy. We never ran in the same crowd."

It was hard to keep my face still and not jerk up to look at Cephus when I knew everyone, including Granny, was watching my every movement.

I held my phone. I hoped they thought I was texting someone, but I quickly typed in the notes to check into Leotta and Terk's relationship. How long had it been going on? What was Terk's relationship with Cephus? How did Mary Anna feel about her mom and Terk? The answers to these questions seemed like a good place to start.

Leotta's eyes slid from me to Granny. Softly, she said, "The kids and I haven't heard a thing from Cephus. I guess he might have drank himself crazy."

Drank? Crazy? I made another note in my phone before I looked up to see the expression on Cephus's face, but he was gone.

"Bless your heart, Leotta." Granny gave Leotta the Southern blessed curse phrase. She plucked a ZULA FAE FOR MAYOR pin from her pocket and stuck it right on Leotta's dress. "You know I appreciate your support."

"Now, Zula Fae." Bea Allen cackled. Her frizzy hair swayed back and forth. "I think Leotta might be voting for O'Dell." Bea Allen leaned over and nudged Leotta with her elbow. "Isn't that right, Leotta?"

"I'm not sure who I'm voting for just yet." Leotta shrugged.

"As if it was a question?" Granny's left eye twitched, letting me know she was keeping something to herself. Granny snatched the pin off Leotta and threw it back in her plastic Ziploc. "I don't waste material on someone who can't make up her mind." Granny pushed back her chair and jumped up. "Let's go, Emma Lee."

"It was nice seeing you again, Leotta. Nice to meet you, Bea Allen." I gave a slight wave that Granny wouldn't see.

If she had seen me give any loyalty to Bea Allen Burns, she'd hold a grudge for the week.

"You too, honey," Bea Allen said loudly, and grinned.

Granny jerked around, giving me the stink-eye.

Bea Allen looked at Granny and grinned again, knowing that she had gotten Granny's goat.

Little did she realize, she only fueled Granny's fire even more.

Chapter 5

"The nerve of Leotta Hardy, saying she doesn't know who she is voting for." Granny huffed the whole way back to the funeral home. "I even took her a Kentucky Hot Brown casserole and blueberry cobbler when that no-good drunk of a husband of hers left her and them babies."

I kept my mouth shut. If I would have agreed, nodded, or even smiled, that was a cue for her to continue.

"That was my good recipe too." She poked my ribs. Her face was as red as the hair on her head. "You know the one where I make the crust and do not use that store-bought kind. I mean *home-made*." Granny's trap kept going. "I don't think she even gave back that casserole dish. You know, the large glass one." Her brows lifted and her hands showed the size of the dish. "Artie's never has them in stock anymore."

"Wait." I stopped right in front of Pose and Relax and grabbed Granny's arm. "Did you say drunk?"

"What? No." Granny shook her head. "Glass casserole dish."

"Back up," I said, and moved out of the way of the Pose and Relax door because a yoga class was letting out. "You called Cephus a drunk."

"I only call it as I see it." Granny lifted her chin in the air like she was above the gossip.

"What do you mean?" I leaned in and asked.

I knew he was considered a drunk, but I wanted to hear what Granny had to say about him and if it would lead me to any clues to why or who killed him.

"He was a drunk. He was always hitting on women. Always at the Watering Hole. And I heard that their marriage wasn't the best. Now"—Granny dug her fingers into my arm—"I'm not spreading no gossip." She straightened her shoulders and tugged on the hem of her shirt. "A good Southern woman doesn't do that."

"Of course you aren't." I grinned.

We both knew she was. I did make a mental

note to check out the information she had handed me on a silver platter.

Booze and womanizing could definitely be a motive for murder.

If Cephus Hardy was the drunk Granny said he was and a womanizer, there were probably plenty of people who wanted him dead. Jealous lovers. Leotta. Husbands. The list was endless. But who? Where did I start?

On our way back to Eternal Slumber, Granny stopped at the old building next to the funeral home. Hettie Bell had been using Granny's front porch and the town square for her yoga classes up until recently. She now rented the old building and had opened Posed and Relax.

"Good morning, ladies." Hettie Bell stood in the doorway of the yoga studio with her arms stretched high in the air before she swept them down to the ground to touch her toes.

She wore tight black yoga pants and a small cross-tee hot pink yoga top, which stood out against her olive skin and chin-length black hair.

I cringed; just watching her do that made my back ache.

"Campaigning already?" She popped up and ran her fingers down her blunt bangs. "It's early."

"Yes we are." Granny pulled out a button and,

with a shaky hand, she held it out. "This will match your outfit perfectly."

"Zula, are you okay?" There was concern in Hettie Bell's voice. She held Granny's hands in hers. "Are you using those breathing exercises I gave you?"

"I have." Granny pulled her hands away from Hettie Bell's grip and rubbed her neck. "But I could use a little downtime."

"Great!" I jumped at the chance to get away from Granny. "You go in there with Hettie and do a little downward dog while I get back to work."

"I am getting ready to begin the Auxiliary women's class." Hettie nodded toward the red Cadillac that was pulling up to the curb.

Beulah Paige. I groaned and took a deep breath.

Mable Claire was sitting in the passenger side with a tight grip on her purse as though someone were going to hijack the car. I walked over to the car and opened the door. Mable Claire pulled her purse closer to her body.

"What's wrong with you, Mable Claire?" I asked, and held the door wide open so she could get out.

"Well . . ." Her soft voice left her soft body. Her pockets jingled when she stepped out of the car. ". . . I heard you might be sick again."

A shadow of annoyance crossed my face when I looked over at Beulah Paige and her red cheeks.

"Beulah Paige, why do you want to go around spreading gossip?" I asked, and bit my lip. If I didn't, I'd come unglued, and they'd really think I was going crazy. "I'm not sick. I was . . ." I stalled for time. " . . . trying out my new Bluetooth."

"Bluetooth, huh?" Beulah Paige asked suspiciously. "Where is it?" She tilted her perfectly coifed head to the left and to the right, trying to get a look at my ears.

"It didn't work very well inside the store, so I had to run out to get good reception," I lied.

"Doc Clyde said that you said Cephus Hardy was back in town." Beulah wasn't going to let it die. She ran her fingers through her red hair like she was stoking the fire. "When I saw Leotta at Higher Grounds, I thought it might be possible he was back. But when I asked her about it, she was so confused. She had no idea what I was talking about."

"I was talking to Mary Anna, and Doc Clyde was eavesdropping." I shrugged. "I'm sure you can understand eavesdropping."

Beulah Paige huffed past me and stuck the key fob over her shoulder, clicking away as her fancy car beeped to let her know it was locked.

My phone chirped a text. It was Mary Anna asking if I was at the funeral home because she'd left her good scissors in the morgue and needed to get them before she headed to work at Girl's Best Friend Spa.

As Beulah sashayed right on into Pose and Relax, she warned Granny, "You need to get a handle on that granddaughter of yours. Come on, Mable Claire."

Mable Claire did as she was told and the two of them disappeared into the yoga studio.

It would be a perfect time to slip in some questions about Cephus to Mary Anna if I could just shake Granny.

"Go on and be with your friends. I'll come by later to help out with the dinner crowd before my romantic dinner date with Jack Henry," I assured her. "Besides, I have to let Mary Anna in the freezer to get her scissors before she goes to work."

"Here." Granny handed me her Ziploc bag of ZULA FOR MAYOR pins. "Tell her to put these on her clients at the hair salon."

"Fine." I grabbed the bag and headed next door to Eternal Slumber.

"Mornin', Emma Lee." John Howard Lloyd stood on the front lawn, scratching his wiry hair.

I tried not to look at the dirt crammed under his fingernails. But it wasn't possible. He had a large shovel in one hand and a two-by-four in the other.

"What are you doing?" I asked.

Seeing him with a shovel and wood wasn't out of the ordinary since he worked for me as the gravedigger, but seeing him with these items in the front yard of Eternal Slumber had me intrigued.

"I'm fixin' to put up an election sign for Zula Fae. Just tryin' to figure out where to put it." He set the shovel and wood on the ground and tucked his hands in the tops of his overalls. "She said she cleared it with you, not that she was telling the truth."

"She did." I pointed to the middle of the yard. "You can stick it in the middle."

He nodded and grabbed the equipment, making his way to the middle of the yard.

"I'll be glad when this election is over!" Mary Anna yelled out the window of her car. She pulled the silver convertible classic Mercedes into the driveway of Eternal Slumber. "I was mobbed by O'Dell's sister and my momma this morning before I even had my boobs tucked in."

She got out of the car, slammed the door and tugged up her V-neck purple shirt, which was tightly tucked into her snug white jeans. Her purple high heels clicked up the sidewalk of the funeral home. Her short bleach-blond hair was neatly tied under a purple, polka-dotted scarf. Mary Anna always tried to dress exactly like her favorite icon, Marilyn Monroe. Even Girl's Best Friend Spa was decorated and dedicated to the famous actress. There was a huge portrait of Marilyn covered in diamonds, her mouth spread open in a breathy grin to greet you as soon as you walked into the spa.

"Well, I'm adding to your stress." I handed her the bag of pins Granny had asked me to give her. "Granny wants you to pass these out at the spa."

"Hmm . . ." Mary Anna reluctantly took the bag and gave me the wonky eye. "Are you asking me as my boss?"

"Nope." I shook my head. "Just a favor to Granny."

"Fine." She wiggled her way past me and proceeded up the steps. I followed her. "I can't believe I forgot my scissors here last night. But my momma called telling me that Teddy was coming to town, and I was so excited, I lost all my marbles."

"Teddy is coming in?" I asked, knowing that I needed to talk to him too but wasn't sure how I was going to.

He had left Sleepy Hollow right after high school to pursue his career in amateur wrestling and I hadn't heard anything about him since.

"Yes. Momma got all geared up like a pocket watch." She patiently waited as I took my key out and opened the door. "Teddy hasn't been the same since Daddy left us and I can't wait to see him."

"I didn't leave!" Cephus appeared and jumped in the air with his elbow coming down like he was doing a pile driver on someone. "I was murdered! I would never leave you, baby girl. Tell her! Tell her, Emma Lee."

"I'm sure it took a toll on Teddy." I pinched my lips together.

Cephus darted back and forth, flailing his arms around.

"Tell her!" he begged one last time until he realized I was ignoring him.

"You haven't heard from Cephus?" I asked, and held the front door open for her. We walked into the vestibule and stood for a minute.

Not to make it so obvious that I was asking questions, I pretended to be busy by fluffing the red-velvet drapes that hung from the large, old windows.

"Not a word." There was sadness in her voice. "I never would have thought Daddy would have left us like that."

"Did he have a reason to leave town?" I walked over near one of the doors of the viewing rooms and straightened the memorial cards sitting on the pedestal.

"None that we could figure." She untied the scarf and gently lifted it off her head. Today she wore her hair in a slick bob with the ends flipped up. "Of course he and Momma had their demons, but nothing we couldn't work out."

"Demons?" That didn't sound good.

"I love your momma," Cephus groaned. He was sitting in one of the winged-back leather chairs in the corner of the vestibule, with his face buried in his hands. "I didn't have any demons."

"You know." We made our way back to the elevator. Mary Anna pushed the DOWN button to take us to the basement, where the morgue was located. "Daddy did drink his weight in beer."

"I could use an ice-cold Stroh's right now." Cephus smacked his lips together and stood right between Mary Anna and me as we rode the elevator down.

"Momma worried about money, Daddy drank it away." Mary Anna kept her hands busy by rolling the scarf around her fingers.

"I took care of y'all," Cephus whined.

"I'm sure he took good care of you." I wanted to make him feel a little better. There was nothing sadder than to see him listen to her talking about him and her not knowing he was there.

"He did, in his own way." She looked up at me. The edges of her eyes turned down. She said, "Sometimes it's been easier with him gone though. Momma hasn't had to worry about money since. And now that she's dating."

The elevator bell dinged and the doors opened.

"Dating! She is dating that sonofabitch Terk Rhinehammer. I knew it when I saw his car parked in front of that fancy coffee shop." Cephus stormed out of the elevator, wringing his hands together. He pretended to have someone in a headlock and giving a noogie. "And my boy. He's a big-time wrastler?"

"Teddy is a big-time wrastler?" I asked

"Wrastler?" Mary Anna cackled. "I haven't heard that since my daddy was around."

"I mean wrestler." Oh, Lordy. I was starting to sound like Cephus Hardy. "Is he a professional now?"

"He does the small venues and is working his way up to the big-time WWE." There was pride on her face. Her red lips curled into a smile. "Daddy would be so proud of him. He loved going to Teddy's matches. He even helped Teddy come up with his signature move."

"Signature move?" I asked.

"Yeah." She smiled. "I'll show you."

"Okay, but don't hurt me." I was a bit cautious.

She wrapped her arm around my head and rested my chin in her elbow. She stuck her other hand around the other side of my head and wrapped her arms together like a bow. She did a little squeeze.

"It's sort of like a sleeper hold but Daddy and Teddy came up with a spin to it." She dropped her arms, letting me out of her grip. "Now it's a move—the Teddy Bear Hold."

"Really?" I was impressed.

"Daddy would love that." She took a deep inhale.

That was pretty impressive. Not many people can say something was named after them. Not anyone I knew.

"Morning, ladies." Vernon Baxter was hard at work on a client in the basement.

Vernon was a stately-looking older man with white hair and a sprinkle of pepper. His steel-blue eyes and debonair good looks reminded me of old Hollywood. I felt like I was standing between Marilyn Monroe and Cary Grant.

He was a retired doctor who performed all the autopsies in Sleepy Hollow. He used Eternal Slumber as his office. We had recently acquired the latest equipment and technology in the mortuary business when the town council voted to use some of the extra tax money to fund the upgrade. Things like the latest in DNA equipment to help the police solve crimes and some more real fancy technology that I didn't even try to understand but Vernon did.

"How's it going?" I asked Vernon about his latest victim.

"Everything's as it seems." He smiled and continued looking around the body lying on the cold, metal table.

I try not to look at the clients when they are not dressed and without full makeup. That did give me the heebie-jeebies. You'd think a ghost would freak me out, but they didn't. Their appearance was just like I remembered them. And that was *a-okay* with me.

"What are you two doing?" He glanced up.

I got a chill when I noticed the bone saw in his hand. The handle of the saw looked like the butt of a gun and the saw part was just that.

"I forgot these." Mary Anna stood next to her makeup station and picked up her scissors. "My best ones."

"That's a little gross." I shivered at the thought. "Do your clients know that?"

"Nope. Dead or living, neither know." She laughed so loud, I held on to the table just in case she did wake the dead and they decided to visit me.

"Say, I hear Bea Allen is in town and staying with Leotta," Vernon said.

He didn't look up as he hacked away on something. I didn't know what it was he was sawing, but I could hear it.

"You know Momma." Mary Anna's tone caught my attention. "She always did have a good friend in Bea Allen. Especially when you four used to double-date."

Did Vernon Baxter know Leotta? I was on high alert to help get Cephus to the other side. Every single conversation was on my radar. No stone unturned was my Betweener motto.

Double date? As far as I knew, Vernon Baxter had been a bachelor all his life, and to my knowledge, he hadn't been dating. Evidently not. I took my cell out of my pocket and typed in a note to check on this double-date thing and if Vernon dated Bea Allen. Not that dating Bea Allen would contribute to finding out who killed Cephus, but it was good gossip to talk to Granny about. Any gossip about the O'Dells was good gossip. Especially here during election time.

Cephus walked over to Vernon. He raised his hand and scratched his chin.

"Vernon Baxter killed me!" Cephus protested, and took a good swing at Vernon.

Not only did my mouth drop, so did my cell phone.

"Are you okay?" Vernon jumped around and rubbed his chin as if he could feel the sting of the punch from Cephus's fist.

I swooped down and picked it up. Luckily, it didn't shatter. I put it back in my pocket and took a deep breath.

"Are you okay?" I asked Vernon, who was still rubbing his chin.

"Suddenly my mouth hurts." He jutted his jaw backward, forward, side to side.

"Earache. I always get jaw pain when I'm getting an earache." Mary Anna insisted on being the doctor in his diagnosis.

"True," he mumbled while rotating his bottom lip. "I should probably stop by Doc Clyde's office."

"Next time I'm really gonna hurt ya!" Cephus danced on his toes with his fists loosely tucked with his thumb and his pinky finger sticking out, jabbing in the air.

"Look at the time." Mary Anna checked out her gold watch with the glittery rhinestones. Mary Anna was always sparkly. "I'm going to be late. I had to double-book a couple perms today since I had a stylist quit on me. Said she'd make more money at a real spa." Mary Anna rolled her eyes and batted her fake lashes. "Real spa. Nothing more real than what I got. Plus you learn a lot." She wiggled her perfectly waxed brows. "If you know what I mean."

"Oh, I know." I walked out with her but not without glancing back at Vernon.

Cephus was gone again. Which was better. I could ask Mary Anna a few more questions without him interrupting. Plus, I might be able to go back down and fiddle around the freezer so Vernon could talk to me.

"Vernon and Bea Allen, huh?" I slid the question between the silence and pushed the elevator key.

"Momma always said they were a strange pair." She gestured with the scissors in her hand.

"How so?"

"Did you see her? Frizzy hair and shit." Mary Anna did spirit fingers around the top of her head. "I was dying to get my hands in that hair of hers. I can do wonders with frizz. You've seen Hettie Bell. I got her crazy hair under control."

She was right. When Hettie Bell came to town, she was gothic-looking, with some big frizzy hair. Eventually, she cleaned her act up and now she has that great yoga studio. She claims she's making Sleepy Hollow Zen, one resident at a time. I've yet to see any results.

"In fact, when I was a kid, Teddy had all that hair just like Daddy." She reminded me of Teddy and the questions I needed answered.

"Oh, yeah!" I had forgotten all about his crazy hair. I'd never seen a white boy with an Afro.

"Well, I used to pin him down and pretend it was Bea Allen's. I swear that was when I decided to become a hairdresser." She elbowed me right as the elevator door opened into the vestibule. "No way could I pin that boy down now. I can't wait for you to see him."

"Are you having a get-together?" I wanted to make sure I did see him.

"We will be over at the carnival tomorrow night. You going?" she asked.

"Good morning." Charlotte Rae darted past us and down the hall, disappearing into her office without even waiting for our response.

"Good to see you too." Mary Anna's nose curled. "Anyway, you going?"

"Yes. Of course. Jack Henry and I wouldn't miss

it for the world." I waved her off and shut the door behind her.

I took my phone out of my pocket and texted Jack Henry.

How is the goat situation? Working on the case I told you about earlier.

Quickly he texted back: *Leave it to the police, Emma Lee!*

I responded: *You worry about the living and the goats. I'll worry about the dead!*

I dipped my head into Charlotte Rae's office to see what her hurry was. Not that I wasn't in a hurry. I was. I needed to get on some of these leads to help Cephus to the other side, starting with figuring out who did him in and where they put him.

"What's the hurry?" I asked her when I opened up the door.

She stood by the window with her back to me. Her long legs looked much longer in her black skirt suit and black heels. Her long red hair draped down her back in the most beautiful curls. She was blessed with Grandpa Raines's genes and Granny's pretty hair. I was cursed with Granny's side of the family. Short and average, but had the Raines's dull brown hair.

Charlotte was good at running the financial

side of the funeral-home business. Like consoling the family, helping them pick out the casket, giving them the options on funerals and paying the funeral-home bills.

I was good at making sure the arrangements ran smooth and the burial was flawless.

"I'm not sure how I'm going to handle that sign out front." Slowly she turned around. An angry gaze rose on her face. "Granny has taken it a bit too far this time. People aren't going to vote for her if she's not going to take this seriously."

"It's just a sign." I rolled my eyes. "You can't go around forgetting where it is that you come from now that you live in the next town over and in that big house."

When Granny gave us the funeral home, Charlotte refused to live here like we had all our life. I stayed. It was perfect for me. How many people could say that they literally rolled out of bed for work?

Not Charlotte. She had wanted to get out of Sleepy Hollow all her life. Now she's just partly out.

"Little sign?" Her voice rose and she pointed out the window. I followed her long, thin fingers down to her perfectly-pink-painted nails to the outside world. "Did you see it, *Emma Lee*?"

"Oh how bad can it be?" I asked, and left her office. I was going to go outside and see it for myself.

"Oh. My. God." It was the second time my mouth dropped today.

The sign was *that bad* and *that big*. It took up the entire front yard. I walked down the front steps of the porch and stepped over a few, like ten, extension cords that were all plugged into one another, then in the outside outlet. I made my way around to the front.

VOTE FOR ZULA FAE RAINES PAYNE flashed in big red lightbulbs. The backdrop was a picture of the United States flag and she had a motto scrolled along the bottom.

You let me take care of your loved ones, let me take care of you!

"What's wrong?" John Howard's wrinkles on his forehead creased. "You said in the middle."

Chapter 6

Granny?" I stomped up the steps of the Sleepy Hollow Inn. "Granny!"

After seeing the sign, I had jumped in the hearse and driven around the square to the Inn. Normally I'd just run across the square, but the carnies were setting up for the carnival and I didn't feel like running around them.

I let the screen door slam behind me when I walked into the Inn. A couple of guests were in the room on the right, eating some of the hors d'oeuvres and drinking her famous sweet tea.

Their heads turned at the sound of the screen door's smacking the frame.

Granny rushed out of the kitchen and down the hall, wiping her hands on her apron.

"What in the world is wrong with you today?" She grabbed me by the arm and jerked me toward the kitchen. "First you go all nuts at Artie's and now you are screaming your way into the Inn."

"Did you see the sign you had John Howard put up in the yard of the funeral home?" I pointed over my shoulder. Granny just kept dragging me.

Once we got into the kitchen she flung me in front of her, letting go.

"Emma Lee, if you don't hide that crazy, Doc Clyde is going to admit you." She shook her finger at me. "I asked you if I could put the sign in the yard and you said yes. Did you forget it already? It was only about an hour ago."

"Granny." I rubbed my arm. Even though I was an adult, she didn't mind taking over when my parents up and retired. Not missing a beat to tell me when I was wrong. "I said a sign. Not a bill-board."

The smell of fresh-baked bread filtered through the air, along with something a little sugary.

"Oh, honey. That was the smallest size. I could've gone bigger." She snapped her fingers. "When your grandfather bought the land for Eternal Slumber, we had an option to buy the land Pose and Relax is on. I wish we had, but that Mamie Sue was a little stingy."

"Who?" I had never even heard of this Mamie Sue.

"Mamie Sue Preston." Granny waved her hand and did the sign of the cross like she was Catholic. We weren't. Not a Catholic church in town.

"Never mind her, she's dead. But if I did own the land where Pose and Relax is, my sign would've been a lot bigger than the little one that's on the lawn now."

"You are telling me that you knew it was that big? Because if you are, you are going to have to answer to Charlotte. She's freaking out," I said. "Gross." My nose curled when I saw the bowl full of some sort of barley, berries, peas and some other sort of oats. "I hope you aren't serving that for breakfast."

Granny ignored me and poured me a big glass of tea and set it on the table.

"Have a seat." She gestured and walked over to the oven. She used the lime-green oven mitts to pull something out of the oven. With the large steel spatula, she scooped up her homemade oatmeal cookies and arranged them on a pretty china plate with little flowers around the edges. "Here."

She put one in front of me.

"You aren't going to win this one with an oatmeal cookie." I lifted my chin in the air, trying not to smell the deliciousness that was put in front of me.

"Fine." She plunked another one down from the plate in her hand. "What about two?"

She didn't wait for my answer before she headed out the door with the smell trailing behind her.

I gobbled them up and poured a second glass of tea before she made it back.

"Better now?" Granny lifted her brow, a slight grin tipping the edges of her lips.

"You always knew how to bribe me." I took another gulp of tea to clear my palate. "Seriously. All the flashing lights? And the motto? I took care of your loved ones, let me take care of you?"

"It's a good one, right." Granny was proud of her play on words. "Me and the Auxiliary gals came up with all sorts of mottos."

"I'm sure you did." I took another long sip. I still wasn't sure how I was going to handle the whole sign thingy. "Don't you think the sign is a bit much?"

"Is the Statue of Liberty too much? What about Mount Rushmore? Is that too much?" Her face contorted, flushed as red as her hair.

"Those are icons of the United States."

"I'm an icon in Sleepy Hollow." She straightened herself up. "I had the idea to open the caves for tourism. I alone turned this downward-spiraling economy into one of the thriving cities in Kentucky. What has O'Dell done? He didn't do nothing. In fact, he voted against my proposal of opening the caves." She opened the junk drawer. Items spilled out onto the floor as she searched around, finally pulling out a pen and paper. "I need to write that down. I forgot all about that."

She scribbled away. She was right. O'Dell really didn't want the visitors to come explore the caves. What had he done for the community?

"You're right!" I pounded my fist on the table. "You do deserve to be mayor and Charlotte is going to have to suck it up."

"Good for us." Granny leaned down and hugged me. I patted her arms. "I'll leave it up to you to tell her."

"Of course you will." I rolled my eyes. "Granny, what do you know about Terk Rhinehammer?"

It seemed like a good question to start with. I needed to go visit Terk and try to figure out if he and his relationship with Leotta had anything to do with Cephus's murder.

"Not much. Terk Rhinehammer and Cephus ran around with a different crowd when your daddy was growing up." She looked at me. Her brow twitched. "Cephus might've stopped to visit every now and then, but not Terk."

"Granny, tell me." I coaxed her to tell me what she was hiding.

"You know, idle gossip." She looked me up and down. Slowly she shuffled over to me. "I guess you are big enough to know stuff."

"Big enough?" I laughed. "I am a big girl and an adult by law."

"Well, kids can be cruel and hurt other kids. But since you and Mary Anna are big kids, I'm sure you'll keep this to yourself." Granny eased down next to me. "I had heard, just heard now"—Granny tried to make gossip sound better—"when Cephus lost his job, I heard Terk had given him a job down at the water plant. If I can recall, I believe Terk was the manager down there. But like I said, he ran around in a different crowd." Her face turned serious. "Them Rhinehammers are Burns people."

Granny liked to classify families into two groups. Burns or Eternal Slumber, depending on what funeral home the families chose to bury their loved ones. In this case, the Rhinehammers must have always used Burns Funeral to bury their people.

"I think it caused a lot of problems between Leotta and Cephus because I had heard that

Leotta didn't want handouts and if Cephus didn't drink so much, he'd have been able to stay in construction."

"Construction?" I realized I had no idea what Cephus had done for a living.

"And I never would have pegged Leotta and Terk together, but I just can't shake the image I saw today." Granny's lips turned up like she had the biggest secret. "When I went to yoga this morning, in the middle of plank pose, I lifted my head and looked out the window overlooking the street. Terk Rhinehammer's big Buick drove right on by, with Leotta Hardy driving." She nodded. "Saw it with my own eyes."

"And she didn't say a word about it when I asked her." I found it interesting that Leotta was trying to hide it.

"Not a word," Granny said. "She looked shocked that you knew it was his. How did you know it was his?"

"Lucky guess." I shrugged. "Where does Terk live?" I asked. I could feel her staring at me. "I'm just wanting to try to understand the dynamics between Leotta and him since I do work with Mary Anna and all."

"Has she been talking about it?" Granny poured herself a glass of tea.

"Well"—I leaned in on my elbows as if I was telling her a big secret—"they are having a big family gathering tomorrow night at the carnival. Mary Anna said Teddy is coming into town. I can't help but wonder if Leotta is going to bring Terk as her boyfriend or something. Besides, he is a voter."

I held the glass up to my lips, lifted my brows and peered over the top at Granny, who was contemplating every word I was saying.

"A vote is a vote." Granny's eyes narrowed.

"What if I pack up some of those cookies and take them over to Terk's for a little campaigning?" The idea was solid. I could pretend to be going door-to-door handing out buttons to get in front of him.

"You are brilliant, granddaughter!" Granny jumped up. She searched the cabinets for some Tupperware and stacked some cookies in it. "This is exactly why I gave you Eternal Slumber."

She shoved the box toward me.

"One more thing." I knew it was going to be a shocker of a question. "What do you think *really* happened to Cephus Hardy?"

"I think he drank himself to death somewhere." Granny never said anything she didn't mean. "I think he got tired of all of Leotta's bullshit and decided to get out."

"Bullshit?" I asked. "What bullshit?"

"Stop talking like that," Granny warned. There were things that always seemed okay for her but were never okay for me. Swearwords were one of them. "Leotta was always stringing along some man around Cephus to get his goat."

"That's right, Zula Fae." Cephus appeared. He leaned on the counter near the cookie sheet. "I'd love to have a cookie and an ice-cold Stroh's."

"Leotta might be all sweet, but she is the jealous type and she's still a woman. Likes to be center of attention. At least that is what I was told." Granny pushed the box of cookies a little closer to me.

Granny pulled back. "Why all these questions? This don't have nothing to do with my campaign, does it?"

"I want to make sure you are nowhere near this mess in the past since Bea Allen Burns has come back to help her brother beat you." I shook my head. "When in politics, the past has a habit of rearing its ugly head."

"Trust me." Granny jabbed her finger in her own chest. "I never ran around with that group. Nor did I do anything in my past that would keep me from winning this election."

Chapter 7

There were two things Southerners hated to see knocking on their door. Jehovah Witnesses, because the majority of us were Baptist, and the undertaker. It was understandable that when Terk Rhinehammer opened the door, his face turned white as all the blood was drained from it after he looked past me and saw my hearse.

"What's wrong?" He used his hands to pat down his chest. "I'm not dead, am I?" he half-heartedly joked.

"You gonna be!" Cephus had a habit of appearing at the wrong times. Which happened to be when he wanted to fight someone.

Cephus bounced on his toes, jabbing the air.

Ahem. I cleared my throat to try to get Cephus to stop. He was becoming a bit of a distraction.

"Can I get you a beer?" The cigarette nestled in the corner of Terk's mouth bounced up and down with every word.

Terk looked different from what I remember when I was a little girl and seeing him around Sleepy Hollow. Granted, that was a lifetime and headful of hair ago, but still, time had not been good to him. His muscular build had turned to flab, especially under his chin, and his long ponytail had turned into a long, thin crown around the bald spot.

"No thank you." I couldn't help but notice the beer gut he had developed from the consumption of the drink in his hand.

"It's noon." He joked. He took the cigarette out of his mouth and took a swig out of the Pabst Blue Ribbon can before he crushed it and threw it in the plastic trash can outside the door. "If I ain't dead, and no one I know isn't, what's the pleasure?"

"I was wondering if I could take a few minutes of your time to talk with you about the election, and my granny, Zula Fae . . ." I held out one of Granny's buttons.

"I know who your granny is." He pulled his

pants clear up to his armpits. His eyes filled with surprise. "Say, are you Bo Raines's kid?"

Now we were getting somewhere. Granted, it wasn't about Cephus, but I was going to hear how he knew my daddy.

"We ain't here to talk about Bo." Cephus stomped. "Take the beer! Hell, I'll take any beer!"

"Do you know my daddy?" I asked, rolling up on my toes and trying to take a gander into his trailer.

He stepped in front of me with his beer gut and chest jutting out, blocking my view.

"I know of your daddy. We never ran around the same circles. That whole funeral gig y'all got going kinda gave me and my buds the creeps." He crossed his arms in front of him. "I'm thinking about voting for O'Dell Burns. He has never tried to bury someone who didn't have pre-need arrangements. Or dig up the dead."

"Well, to be fair." I put my hands on my hips. Terk made it sound like Eternal Slumber was a fly-by-night funeral parlor. "Granny was married to Earl Way and Chicken Teater hadn't died of pneumonia but had been murdered so Sleepy Hollow's finest began working on his case and needed clues. All legitimate reasons."

I had to admit that Eternal Slumber had taken a few hits over the years. It wasn't good for business when Granny's second husband died and she laid him out right in the front viewing room of Eternal Slumber with the entire town there to pay their respects, or be nosy. Either way, they were there when Earl Way's ex-wife and Granny's number one nemesis, Ruthie Sue Payne, showed up with O'Dell Burns and plucked Earl Way's dead body right out of his casket.

Earl Way never took care of updating his funeral needs when he married Granny, leaving O'Dell Burns with the most current funeral arrangements. Ruthie didn't care, she just wanted to get under Granny's skin. Only Granny put on a brave face and smiled like a good Southern woman . . . hiding her crazy, just like me.

Then there was Chicken. He too had come to see me, and he was who sent Cephus to me. Everyone thought he died of pneumonia. Everyone was wrong. He was murdered and I had to help him to the other side.

Cephus's case was a little different than the last two. There was no body. No evidence he was murdered. Somehow, I had to find his body. Had he been murdered five years ago? Would there be any bones or anything left of him?

I glanced over at Cephus. His eyes never left Terk. Terk's eyes never left me. Cephus wrung his hands and used his finger to rotate the ring on this right-hand ring finger.

"Do you wear that all the time?" I pointed.

"Never take it off." Cephus held his hand up in the air, showing me the gold band and square onyx stone that took up the entire face of the ring.

"Wear what?" Terk snubbed out his half-smoked cigarette on the ground with his foot.

"Nothing." I shook my head, realizing I had said that out loud. "Anyway, I don't see a car." I had to slip in Leotta somehow. "I'd be more than happy to come pick you up so you could vote. Voting is a privilege every citizen needs to exercise no matter if you vote for Granny or not."

"What makes you think I don't have a car?" he snarled.

"I don't see one." I twirled around and took a good look at his small yard.

"My friend has my old Buick. I've got a ride."

"You mean Leotta Hardy?" I asked.

His head jerked up. "How do you know about Leotta?"

It wasn't like I could tell him that Cephus Hardy was dead and right there about to give him the smackdown, nor could I tell him that I had seen his old Buick parked in front of Higher Grounds when I acted like I had no idea he had a car and offered him a ride.

"Isn't she still married to Cephus Hardy?" My eyes zeroed in on his facial expression.

Cephus jumped around me and grabbed Terk by the neck. "Yeah, you sonofabitch!"

"Stop!" I yelled, but it was too late. Terk was feeling the effect of Cephus's revenge.

Terk choked out a lung, bent over and continued to hack.

"Need. A. Beer," he gasped, holding one hand up to his throat and the other pointed into the trailer.

I rushed past him and made a sharp right turn into the kitchen, where there was a round café table, two chairs, a small counter with a sink and a few upper cabinets that had yellowed from the cigarette smoke.

There was a piece of paper lying on the table with Cephus Hardy printed big and bold at the top. Without even looking at it and without thinking, I grabbed it and stuck it in my pocket.

I picked up a glass from the wire drying rack on the counter next to the sink and turned on the faucet to fill it with water before I rushed back out to Terk, who had now gone out on his lawn in a gasping fit and lay on the ground.

Cephus stood next to Terk, laughing his head off and tapping the toe of his white, patent-leather shoe.

"Clearly he didn't want to talk about my girl." Cephus brushed his hands together. "My business here is done."

Terk pointed to the hearse and nodded.

"You want me to take you to Doc Clyde?" I asked.

Up and down his head went. There was a fear of death in his eyes.

"Don't you dare help that thief." Cephus ran alongside me and Terk. I opened the door. Cephus tried to step in front of us, but I tucked Terk inside and slammed the door. "That thief needs to come to my side so I can get him in a real chokehold."

I rushed to the driver's side and jumped in. I threw the hearse in gear and peeled out of the gravel drive, spitting rocks behind me.

"Maybe you should stop smoking." I took the drive over to Doc Clyde's as an opportunity to lecture him on his bad habit. "Or you will be riding back there next time." I pointed to the gurney in the back.

"Awe, he's all right." Cephus sat cross-legged on the gurney. He twirled the ring, using his thumb around his finger. "Let him smoke."

Cephus and I both knew Terk had choked because Cephus did a little ghost kung fu on him, but Terk didn't know that.

Before I could bring the hearse to a full stop Terk jumped out, holding his throat. He didn't look back or even thank me for the ride.

"Sonofabitch." Cephus appeared up front in the passenger seat Terk had vacated. He muttered some other expletive, but I drove off, trying to get the note out of my pocket.

Chapter 8

"Well?" Charlotte was hunkered over her desk when I got back from visiting Terk and taking him to see Doc Clyde. "Did you talk to Granny?"

"I did." I ran my fingers through my hair and leaned up against the doorjamb of her office door. Talking to Charlotte was a lot more stressful than any murdered ghost or dealing with Granny. I held the note in my hand. "She's harmless. I think we can let her keep her sign up. It's just a week away. And we don't have any clients right now."

"Right now is right." Charlotte pushed her chair back, letting it roll into the bookshelf behind her. "We don't know when our clients' time is up.

We don't know when we are going to have clients. What if we get a call in a minute? Then what?"

"I guess we will deal with it then." I shrugged and pushed off the door casing. "I'm going to see Vernon."

"He's gone. He's done with the autopsy and the family has decided to use Burns Funeral. Bea Allen came over here to get him with O'Dell's hearse." Charlotte's face dripped with a look of disgust.

"Well, isn't it your job to talk with the family?" I reminded her of the role she had fought for when Granny retired.

Originally, I thought Charlotte and I would share the duties, all the duties. But Charlotte was too prissy to get her hands dirty. She rarely even went down to the morgue or up to the casket when a client was laid out in the viewing room.

"Since when did Bea Allen come back to town?" Charlotte asked as she picked at the pink polish on her fingernails.

"She's just visiting while the election is going on. I think she's going to do some campaigning for O'Dell. That's why we need the sign." I looked at my watch. Where was the day going? I still needed to get groceries for my romantic dinner with Jack Henry as well as go help Granny with the dinner crowd at Sleepy Hollow Inn. "I've got to go help Granny since she's shorthanded, with Hettie Bell opening up the yoga studio."

I left out the part about me having Jack Henry over for dinner because she wouldn't have seen that as a priority.

"Fine," Charlotte called after me. "But the sign goes down the minute the election polls close! You hear me, Emma Lee? One week! One week!" she screamed from the top of her pretty little head.

There wasn't any need to respond to her rants. Charlotte Rae always thought she was right. It was Momma, Daddy, and Granny's fault for letting her.

I let myself out the front door and decided to take my chances and walk across the square to the Inn. The carnival workers were almost done with setting up a few of the rides. The tilt-a-whirl was minus a few riding buckets, but I was sure I'd be on one tomorrow.

No matter what the age, everyone in Sleepy Hollow loved when the carnival came to town. There were a few tents set up. The one with the stage was where local bands would locate and play a set or two, plus the pergola was all dolled up with flowers for the pageant contestants to walk under. It was the time of the year when all the mommies dolled up their precious little girls in large, fluffy dresses, shiny shoes, big hair bows, high hair and spent all their money on dance lessons all for one little plastic trophy with Queen scrolled on the small silver plate.

Mary Anna had mentioned she was going to be busy doing the hair and makeup for them. She even said something about having to be fast so the little girls didn't lash out and bite her.

I uncurled the note and tried to read it as I walked. There was a bunch of scribble that I couldn't make out, but I clearly read something about a payday and Cephus's collecting it. What did that mean? Payday?

"Emma Lee Raines, you sure have grown up to be a beaut." The carnival guy stood on a ladder working on the dunking booth. "It's me, Digger Spears."

He jumped off and landed on his two feet. A smile crossed his face. He stood around five-foot-six (shorter than me) with a more-than-average muscular build. He wore one of those shirts with a Celtic cross on the front and jeans with man bling on it. Something you'd never see Jack Henry in and that made me glad.

"Digger Spears?" I squinted, recalling the shorter version of this Digger Spears. I put the note back in my pocket. "When did you get back in town?"

Digger and his family had left town when he was in high school. I think it was his senior year, but he was younger than me so I really never paid too much attention, though I did hear his family had moved back to Sleepy Hollow some time later without Digger.

Sleepy Hollow was so small, everyone knew everyone. Even the Digger Spearses of the community.

"I'm a world traveler now." He rocked back and forth on his feet. Pride written on his face. He rubbed his brown, buzzed-cut hair. "I'm working with the carnival. Seen a lot of things. I love it."

"Great for you, Digger." I smiled, trying to hide my reaction to his lack of ambition. But who was I to judge. Maybe I would have joined the carnival if I didn't have the luxury of running the family business. "I'll be seeing you."

I passed by with a wave.

"You do that, Emma Lee." He waved. "Hey, is the Watering Hole still around?"

"It sure is," I said over my shoulder.

"Maybe we can grab a drink while I'm in town," he said.

"We'll see." I continued to walk, knowing good and well that I was going to steer clear of him.

I picked up speed and made it over to the Sleepy Hollow Inn in record time. The rocking chairs on the front porch were taken, which meant I was going to be busy and my hands were going to be really pruned for my date with Jack Henry. A lot of people meant there were a lot of dishes to clean.

"Where have you been?" Granny rushed around the kitchen, juggling different plates as she dipped out food on each one. "I've been running around like a madwoman."

Granny handed over the full plates to one of her servers before she rolled up her sleeves and went knuckle deep into the homemade piecrusts she was making for the desserts.

"First I saved Terk Rhinehammer's life." I threw that in nonchalantly because I knew Doc Clyde would tell her about Terk's choking episode and my involvement. Without her even telling me, I plunged my hands into the soapy, steaming-hot water and began to scrub the glasses that were submerged. "I'm not sure but I think little Digger Spears just hit on me."

"Back up." Granny stopped. She put her hand on the counter and leaned in. Flour flew up in puffs of smoke. "Terk Rhinehammer?"

"Yeah. Remember I went over to his neighborhood to do some campaigning for you." I knew she wasn't going to buy it though it was worth the shot. "And he happened to be choking. He asked me to take him to Doc Clyde. I think he has that smoker's cough. I told him too."

I went through the full routine of dishwashing. Submerge, scrub, submerge again, and run under the water faucet before putting it in the drying rack.

"Well, who is he voting for?" Granny asked.

"I wish I had a clear answer, but he wasn't sure." I wasn't going to tell Granny Terk had mentioned that he was probably going to vote for O'Dell, in fear she would march over to Doc Clyde's and finish off what Cephus had started.

I ran a soapy glass under the water faucet and put it in the drying rack.

"But since I saved his life and drove him to Doc Clyde, I think that means he owes us." I grinned. "One vote for Zula Fae Raines Payne coming up."

"Good girl." Granny kneaded the dough, using her knuckles before flipping it and kneading the other side.

One of Granny's young busboys from the community came in and told her a customer was asking for her.

"I can't go out there. I've got to get these pies

done." She glanced at me. "Emma Lee, dear, go see who's out there."

"Fine." I sighed and dried my hands and followed the kid out to the dining room.

Every table in the place was filled. The entire back wall of the room was ceiling-to-floor glass windows and had an amazing view of the mountainous backdrop and the caves. It was truly spectacular.

"Over there," the boy said.

I followed down his arm and across his pointed finger to a table in the far corner. Leotta Hardy and a man. Someone I didn't recognize. It wasn't Terk Rhinehammer. I thanked the boy and made my way over to Leotta's table.

"Hi, Leotta." I put my hand on the back of her chair and faced the bald man. "Twice in one day. It's so good you are getting out and about."

"I had to pull her teeth to get her here." The voice was familiar but the face wasn't.

"I'm Emma Lee Raines." I put my hand out. "My Granny owns the Inn."

He jumped up and grabbed me, twirling me around like we were long-lost buddies.

"Hell, Emma Lee. I know it's been awhile, but damn. It's me, Teddy." He sat me down and backed up to look at me.

Teddy had turned out to be a big boy. He stood about six-foot-four and weighed a good 250. His neck was as big around as an eighteen-wheeler tire.

"It's my boy!" Cephus appeared in the seat next to Leotta. His arm curled around the back of her chair like they were on a date.

"Gosh, Teddy." My eyes grew. "I didn't recognize you. You have . . ."

"Gotten big!" Cephus's voice escalated. "I never thought that boy was ever gonna grow."

Teddy did a muscle pose with his arms before he did the whole bouncing pectoral move with his boobs. "I'm a wrestling champ. International."

It was hard for me not to stare at each boob taking its turn bouncing up and down.

"Oh." My brows lifted along with my mouth. "Impressive. I'm just the undertaker now. How long are you in town for?"

"I'm here for the carnival." He put his hand on Leotta. "Plus I haven't been able to get home to visit with Momma. And I guess I need to see that sister of mine." He ran his hand over his bald head. "Not for a haircut either."

Leotta's thin lips got thinner as they stretched upward.

"I bet you wished your daddy was here to see

you." The words jumped out of my mouth before I could take them back. Teddy's brows pushed together, creasing the skin between them. "I'm so sorry." I put my hands in front of me. "I'll go get Granny. It sure was nice seeing you Teddy. Bye, Leotta."

"Why you rushing off?" Cephus kept pace with me as I made my way back to the kitchen. "Tell them I'm dead. Tell them I didn't up and leave them. Tell them that Vernon Baxter murdered me."

I ducked into the bathroom; Cephus followed.

"Whhhhhaat?" My heart fell to my feet.

"You heard me. Vernon Baxter killed me." Cephus stood ramrod straight and was serious as a bear on a hunt for food.

"How do you know Vernon Baxter killed you?" I asked in a hushed whisper. Vernon Baxter of all men would be the last suspect on my list. "I've known Vernon for a while now. He wouldn't hurt a flea."

"He did." Cephus's jaw jutted out. Face was serious, hair still kinky curly. He tugged on his polyester taupe pants that ended at the laces perfectly tied on his white, patent-leather shoes. "He was trying to hit on my Leotta. The last thing I remember, I went over to his house. He was out in the garden when I confronted him. He denied it, but I knew he was lying. Leotta had confessed. Straight up told me to my face that she and Vernon had almost knocked boots."

"Knocked boots?" I asked.

"You know." Cephus put his hands out in front of him and gyrated his hips back and forth. "Ump momma, ump momma."

My nose curled and I got all sorts of eww and images I didn't want to have.

"His telephone rang and he went inside the house to get it. Next thing I know . . ." He snapped his fingers and did a little tap dance, ending with his hands and arms in a ta-da. "Here I am. Dead."

"Not only Terk Rhinehammer was after Leotta, but Vernon Baxter too?" I asked, making sure I had it straight in my head.

"Yeppers." He shook his head back and forth, not a curl or hair moved.

"I'll put him on the list." I took my phone out of my pocket and made a note along with the others. The list was getting long and Cephus was on my nerves. I had to get him to the other side before he really did drive me crazy, over the edge, to my breaking point.

"What about that cold Stroh's?" he asked.

"We'll see." I opened the bathroom door just as Granny jumped out of the way.

"Who were you talking to?" There was a pensive shimmer of shadow in Granny's eyes.

"Jack Henry." I put my phone back in my pocket. "We have dinner plans after I'm done here."

"Hmm." Granny was smarter than your average bear. It was almost impossible to get anything by her. "Well, tomorrow night before the carnival, there is going to be a meet-the-candidate cookout for me. The girls"—by girls she meant Auxiliary—"are giving it. I expect you and Charlotte Rae to be there."

"I will be, but I can't promise Charlotte will stick around after work," I warned.

"She better and you tell her I said so," Granny warned before she went out to greet Leotta and Teddy. She turned back around. "Who is that with Leotta?"

"He's my boy and he's a wrastler." Cephus put his hand out to "tap out." I rolled my eyes.

"That's little Teddy." I tilted my head around the corner of the door to get another look. "Can you believe he's not so little anymore? He is some sort of big-time wrastler."

"Wrastler? What's that?" Granny asked.

"Wrestler. Big-time wrestler." I gave her a gentle nudge. "You go find out while I finish up the dishes. You are good at getting the gossip. Plus,

Bea Allen isn't around to try to talk Leotta into voting for O'Dell. Don't forget to ask about Terk. Or Cephus. Go."

The little encouragement about the election was all Granny needed to find out everything I needed to know about Teddy. I wanted to know what they really thought about Cephus's being gone for five years.

It was another half hour before Granny made it back to the kitchen and I finished up the dishes. The Inn's guests were finished dining and ready for their pie, scoop of ice cream, and a refill on their sweet tea or a hot cup of coffee.

"You wouldn't believe the name Teddy has made for himself." Granny took the sharp knife to cut nice and cute every single pie piece perfectly even. "He's a star. Biggest star out of Sleepy Hollow. He's tough as nails and just as sharp."

Granny jumped around, doing some sort of karate move.

"Is that right?" Sarcasm dripped out my mouth. "That was karate. Not wrestling," I pointed out about her move.

Somehow, I doubted Teddy was a star or even smart. At least I hadn't seen him in any of the gossip magazines in the magazine aisle at Artie's nor heard anything about him from Mary Anna until earlier today. Though I dare not tell Granny that. I was in no mood to hear an argument. I had to get to the grocery and get some dinner for me and Jack Henry. Time was ticking.

"Don't believe me?" Granny pointed the knife at me. "I bet you get on that fancy phone of yours and check it out."

"What did he say?" I thought I would appease her for a minute before I got to the good stuff about Terk and Cephus.

"He said that after he graduated, right after Cephus left, he went to Cincinnati, where they do the majority of minor-league wrestling." Granny continued to tell the tale and cut the pies. I followed along, putting a slice on each plate along with a scoop of ice cream. "He said this big manager took to him like a daddy."

"A daddy?" Cephus cried out from behind me. "Teddy has got a daddy. Me!"

I jumped, sending a glob of ice cream soaring through the air.

"What is wrong with you?" Granny growled.

"I'm in a hurry." I nodded up to her clock. "I have a dinner date with Jack Henry and I need to get something to fix."

"Don't you worry. I've got something you can

take." Granny began her tale again. "Anyway . . ." She paused to remember where she left off.

"Like a daddy," I reminded her.

"Daddy my ass." Cephus wrung his hands again. "I'm gonna need that ice-cold Stroh's to keep up with this, Emma Lee. Soon."

I took a deep breath, trying to listen to Granny and tune out Cephus. I was going to need that ice-cold Stroh's to keep my sanity.

"Right, like a daddy. The guy taught him how to do all the right wrestling moves and took him clear out to Calee-fornia." Granny's accent was good at destroying many words. *California* was one of them. "Then he got himself an agent and now he's wrestling all over. Next month he's going to make his big debut at that WWE on TV."

"Is that right?" I asked.

"Pay per view." Granny finished with the last piece of pie and walked over to the freezer. She took something out, put it in an Artie's plastic bag, and put it on the table. "Dinner for you and Jack Henry. All you have to do is nuke it."

"Great." I kissed Granny on the cheek and grabbed the bag. "Wait," I stopped at the door. "What did they say about Cephus and Terk?"

"Teddy fidgeted when I asked Leotta about

Terk. He didn't like it at all." Granny took in a deep breath. "Leotta said that she and Terk were just friends and he let her use his car when she needed to."

"That's my boy." Cephus perked up a little bit.

"Did she say anything about Bea Allen?"

"Emma Lee, I swear. You are getting worse than Beulah Paige. Where are you coming up with all this nonsense?" Granny spat. "Right here at election time too."

"I won't tell if you don't." I winked.

Granny laughed.

In the South, a wink speaks louder than words.

Chapter 9

I had barely gotten home and changed my clothes when Jack Henry came knocking at my door.

If I hadn't taken the long way around the square, I would have made it home ten minutes earlier and gotten the food in the microwave. I didn't want to risk seeing Digger Spears. The way I figured it, Digger would see me and Jack Henry at the carnival and drop the subject of grabbing a beer.

The ten-minute walk did give me time to assess and reassess the list of notes I had taken on my phone. The suspects I thought could have killed Cephus and the suspects he thought had killed him. I kept turning the facts and little snippets of information I had collected from not only myself and Cephus, but from Granny, Mary Anna and Bea Allen. The pieces weren't fitting together like a good little murder mystery. My problem was that it was too early in the investigation game and I was too exhausted to try to figure any more of it out.

"Hey, babe." Jack Henry's slow, Southern drawl made my toes curl, tickling my heart. "I've been wrestling goats all afternoon. I'm starving."

"Good. Me too." I opened the door and took his hat. "How were the goats? Was it baaaaad?"

"Nice impression." Jack Henry bent down and kissed the tip of my nose. "Sanford Brumfield swears someone is letting them out. I even looked at the fence and the gate. Those are some talented goats to be able to get out of those pens."

"Was Dottie Kramer beside herself?" I asked.

Dottie had always lived a life of solitude. She would come into town on Farmer's Market Day, sell her veggies and go back home. She did come to funerals to pay her respect and she was seated in the front row of the Baptist church every Sunday, but other than that, she was pretty much a hermit.

"She was. She said they had ruined her berries and in turn cost her money. Sanford plucked a few hundred from his money clip and handed it to her. He said he'd make good by her. I warned him that if they got out again, he'd face a fine. He assured me they wouldn't get out." Jack Henry smiled. His dimples deepened.

Jack Henry Ross was one of those guys who got better-looking over time. Every time I saw him, my heart did flip flops in my chest. I ran my hands through his brown, high-and-tight cop cut and stared deep into his big brown eyes before I gave him a kiss.

"So"—he stepped in and followed me down my little hall into the small family room—"let's get this over with."

"What?" I shrugged and held up a finger. "I'll be right back. I want to check on dinner."

Charlotte Rae and I had turned the family residence into another viewing room when we took over Eternal Slumber, leaving a little one-bedroom apartment in the rear. It was plenty enough space for me and my needs. There was a bedroom, kitchenette, bathroom, and small television room. I left Jack Henry in front of the TV.

I flipped the light on in the kitchenette and pulled the dinners out of the plastic grocery bag.

"LEAN MEAL?" I read the label of the frozen TV dinner Granny had stuck in the plastic grocery bag.

I knocked on the hard cardboard box with a picture of a flat piece of chicken smothered in some sort of white sauce and pieces of chopped-up asparagus. "Lean Meals?" I asked again, and took out the other Lean Meal Granny thought was good enough for my romantic dinner with Jack Henry.

"How's dinner coming?" Jack Henry walked in and put his arms around my waist. He took a deep inhale before he snuggled in my neck. "Your hair smells like cigarette smoke."

He pulled back. His eyes slid around me and focused on the microwave meals.

"Emma Lee? What is going on?" Jack Henry's eyes hooded like they did when he was on a case. I zipped the cardboard zipper off the side of one of the boxes. "Have you been working on this whole Cephus Hardy notion all day long?"

I ripped the plastic cover off the Lean Meal.

"I'm telling you, Cephus Hardy is dead." I bent down and took a good long whiff of the contents, which were supposed to be chicken. "You and I both know what it means when a ghost comes to visit me. The visits aren't friendly 'hey missing you from Great Beyond' chitchats. Or the big guy from the sky sends his love."

"What is that?" He reached over and flicked the layer of ice that had formed over the top the Lean Meal.

"That's . . ." I bit my lip, "protective covering for the meal. It keeps it good."

"Protective covering? Is that what people are calling freezer burn nowadays?" He chuckled. "I'm not eating that."

"Oh, Jack Henry," I whined. "I really did want to make you a nice meal. I had all the intentions in the world. I had gone to Artie's and that's when Cephus showed up. Nosy Doc Clyde happened to be walking down the magazine aisle and saw me talking to myself, when I was really talking to Cephus."

Jack Henry's jaw and facial features softened. He didn't seem impressed. He knew I was pretty good at disguising my conversations with ghosts. Not this time.

"I thought Cephus had come home." I shrugged. "Of course, I had to get out of there once I realized Cephus was not there in the flesh. And that's when I ran smack-dab into Beulah Paige, who went around telling everyone I had a relapse of the Funeral Trauma, sending Granny into a fit."

"All I said was that I wasn't eating that." He smiled, pointed to the Lean Meal, then gathered me in his arms. "How about we go grab a bite somewhere?"

"Really?" Relief settled in my gut.

"And maybe we can talk about what you found

out today." Jack Henry ran his hand down my arm and took me by the hand, leading me out of the kitchen. "Maybe a beer would do us good."

"Great." I tried to keep a steady face when Cephus appeared right next to Jack Henry.

It was hard not to laugh at Cephus's outfit compared to Jack Henry's.

"Beer?" Cephus danced. He tapped his forehead. "Tonight is wing night at the Watering Hole. You could go there."

I bit my lip and grabbed my purse. I felt my back pocket to make sure I had my cell.

"You can ask questions there. All the guys know me pretty well." Cephus made a compelling argument. "Ask them about Terk, Vernon and Leotta. Dom, dom, dom." He made some good sound effects. "The murder plot thickens even though I know it was Vernon."

"Tonight is wing night at the Watering Hole." Vernon Baxter was far from a killer and I was going to prove that to Cephus once and for all.

"The Watering Hole?" Jack Henry held the door open for me, but not without trying to get his eyes on my face, assessing me like he did a criminal.

I swallowed. "Uh-huh." I didn't make eye contact when I walked past him.

"Oh-kay. The Watering Hole it is." There was no

argument from him. I was sure he knew he probably wouldn't win anyway. "Since we are going that way, why don't we just keep going and head to Bella Vino Ristorante?"

"Tempting. But I'm not feeling like the forty-minute drive," I lied. Driving to Lexington, the closest large town near Sleepy Hollow, was really an enjoyable ride of scenic country roads and beautiful foliage. "And the wait would be long since we don't have a reservation."

Bella Vino was my favorite restaurant. Unfortunately, it wasn't the Watering Hole, where I needed to get answers so I could help Cephus and get my life back.

"Fine." Jack Henry tapped the wheel of the cop car. It was funny how each of us had a company car as our only car. "How did you get the smoke-filled hair?"

"I went to see Terk Rhinehammer." I wasn't sure how much detail I wanted to give him. Like I said, the puzzle pieces of the information I had gathered, or lack thereof, weren't fitting together. I needed more time. "When I went to Higher Grounds this morning, Leotta Hardy was in there and she was driving Terk's car. Since Cephus showed, out of the blue . . ." I glanced to the backseat. Cephus wasn't there. " . . . and Leotta still believes Cephus is living somewhere else, I just thought I would pop by and see what I could find out."

"And he was forthcoming to an undertaker's questions?"

"So I'm not a cop, but I have solved or helped solve a couple crimes. And no." I shook my head. "I used Granny's campaign and buttons to go over there. You know, like asking for his vote."

"Well?" Jack Henry asked.

He turned the car off Main Street and headed down the old country road on the way to the Watering Hole. It was the first stop as soon as you crossed the county line. Sleepy Hollow was in a dry county and that meant no type of liquor or beer sales in any part of the county. The Sleepy Hollow town drunks kept the Watering Hole in business. Smart of the owners to stick it right on the county line.

"Terk opened the door, huffing and puffing, with a beer in his hand and a cig hanging out of his mouth." I turned in my seat to face Jack Henry. "When I asked him questions about his relationship with Leotta Hardy, he got all choked up and fell out into the yard. I had to get him a glass of water and tried to look around." I pulled out the piece of paper I had taken. "I took this."

I held out the paper.

"I am not seeing that." Jack Henry glanced at my hand and looked away. "That's illegal. You stole from his home."

"It's a piece of paper," I quipped. "Maybe I needed to write something down about his medical history when I went out there with my water."

"Is there anything about his medical history on there?"

"No. But I did end up taking him to Doc Clyde's."

"Did he have a heart attack or something?"

"Umm . . . no."

"Why was he choking?"

"Cephus had has hands around his neck." It sounded horrible and I knew it. "I tried to stop him by yelling stop, but I couldn't just flat-out talk to him without someone's seeing me."

"How the hell did a ghost get his hands around a living person's neck?" Jack Henry knew about my gift and believed it because he had taken me to a psychic in Lexington who dealt with unexplained paranormal things. She confirmed that I was a Betweener and they wouldn't leave me alone until I figured out what they wanted.

Unfortunately, my ghost clients wanted me to figure out who murdered them.

"Do you really want me to try to explain?" I asked.

"No, but still. You can't help ghosts who want to go around murdering people who are living. Do you hear that, Cephus Hardy?" Jack Henry yelled to the back of the car.

"He's not here." I grinned at how cute he was being.

"Then you tell him when you do see him," he warned. "Or I won't be helping you put together all these little"—he flailed his hand in the direction of the piece of paper I had taken from Terk's—"clues you seem to find."

"Okay. I'll tell him." I turned back around, putting the piece of paper back in my pants pocket. I could see the half-lit sign of the Watering Hole down the road. It was a large cowboy boot with blinking lights all the way around it. I don't think I had ever seen all the lights lit at once. There was always a burned-out one, few, or several. "Anyway, Cephus seems to think that Terk and Leotta are having an affair, but I'm not so sure."

"If anyone can figure out their relationship, you can. Or Zula Fae." His brows rose and he pulled the car into the gravel lot. He looked out the windshield to find a spot to park. "It's busy tonight."

"Wing night is always busy." Cephus appeared in the back.

"Cephus said wing night is popular." I pointed out the window to an aisle over where there was spot near the motorcycles.

"I thought you said Cephus wasn't here."

"He is now." I unclicked my seat belt and started to get out before Jack Henry put his hand on me.

"Emma Lee, please don't make me give you my speech about how you need to stay out of official police business." He lovingly rubbed my hand. "The little clues are good, but if you find out that Cephus really was murdered, you need to leave it up to the professionals."

"She tried to tell you numbnuts, but you blew her off." Cephus was good with his one-liners.

I laughed out loud.

"What? I'm serious." He jerked his hand away.

"I tried to tell you this morning that Cephus said he was murdered." I had hurt his ego and didn't mean to.

He did care for me and my well-being and safety. It just took a lot more than a ghost to convince him there had been a murder.

"Where is the body? Is he in Sleepy Hollow? What if he did leave and it's out of my jurisdiction? How would I explain that to the authorities?" He put his hands in the air, doing some sort of fairy-dust sprinkling. In a strange, mocking voice, he said, "The ghost of Cephus Hardy says he's been murdered. At least that's what he told my girlfriend ghost-whisperer."

"Stop mocking me." I had become annoyed. "You know I'm serious. Have I ever had a ghost that wasn't murdered come to me for help?"

"Let's go. I'm tired of talking about this. I'm hungry." Jack Henry's demeanor had suddenly turned sour. "Maybe I need food."

"You need a quick kick in the ass," Cephus called from behind us. "That's what you need."

Chapter 10

The Watering Hole was crowded. Even the horse-saddle barstools were taken.

"There's a booth by the pool table." Jack Henry parted the thick cigarette smoke with his pointer finger.

Just then, a couple of people got up from the bar.

"Here!" I yelled over the jukebox and flung my leg over the saddle like I was mounting a horse.

I scooted my butt up and held on to the horn and slid my feet into the stirrups.

Jack Henry didn't make a fuss even though I knew he wanted a booth so we could talk. He just took a seat next to me.

"What'll it be?" the bartender asked, looking directly at Jack Henry.

"We'll have the draft and an order of wings," Jack Henry ordered.

"Wait!" I put my hand out. "I'll have an ice-cold Stroh's." I left off the "h" like Cephus did.

The bartender's lips turned up. A mischievous grin crossed his face. His eyes danced. "An ice-cold Stroh's coming up for you and a draft for you. I'll put the wings in."

"Weee-doggie!" Cephus jumped around, slapping his knees like he had just come back to life. "I can't wait to see that can!"

"What in the world has gotten into you?" Jack Henry put his hands on his knee and slightly shifted his body toward me.

"Nothing. Trying something new." I tore the edges off the bar napkin and rolled the pieces into little balls.

"Are you starting to take on your ghost's eating habits?" Jack Henry had a look of concern on his face.

"Don't be ridiculous. There is no harm," I said.

Jack Henry was beginning to annoy me.

"I wasn't going to say anything, but Zula Fae called me." Jack Henry folded his hands and placed them on the bar top. He looked forward. "I'm worried she might be right this time."

"Really?" I rolled my eyes. "Since when did Zula Fae make any more sense than I do?"

"True, but your behavior with this one is different." By this one, he meant ghost. Cephus Hardy. "You've started sticking your nose in other's business, you're not following leads, you are craving strange foods. And you have been less obvious about disguising your relationship with this one."

"Not true. Not true. Not true." I tapped the counter. "I have only followed leads that Cephus has given me."

That was when I knew, I couldn't tell Jack Henry any more of the clues. Definitely not that Cephus believed Vernon was his killer. And I also knew that I was going to have to keep my mouth shut. Play the good undertaker and just plug along. Only giving Jack Henry solid clues.

Cephus was behind the bar watching the bartender take out the can of Stroh's.

"You know, I haven't had anyone ask for a Stroh's since"—he shook his head—"never mind. It's just the only person I have ever heard come in here asking for an ice-cold Stroh's was . . ." He stopped. He squinted. He pointed. "Are you related to Cephus . . ." He snapped his fingers, trying to remember Hardy.

"Hardy?" Jack Henry finished it for him.

"Yeah." He snapped his fingers again. "That's right. Cephus Hardy. Are you related to him?"

"Something like that." Jack Henry picked up his glass of draft beer and took a swig.

"Get out! Really? Where the hell has he been?" The bartender leaned against the bar and folded his arms. "Did he ever cash in on that big payday?"

"What big payday?" I jumped at the opportunity to ask, recalling the note I had found at Terk Rhinehammer's house.

"Easy." The bartender put his hands in front of me. "He said something about getting his money. I don't know. I figured he'd gotten his big payday and moved."

"What did he specifically say?" I asked. Why hadn't Leotta or anyone else come in here to check to see if anyone knew anything about his disappearance five years ago?

"He said that he was going to be living on easy street and he and his family didn't have to worry about money anymore." The bartender gave us the hold-on finger and went down the line, taking more refill orders.

"See. I told you," I murmured, and popped open my can of Stroh's. "Here's to you." I held the can up in the air toward Cephus.

"Jesus, Emma. Now we are toasting them?" Jack shook his head and took more swigs from his glass.

I took a long drink of the old, sour beer.

"Blah." I stuck my tongue out in disgust. "Who can drink this stuff?"

"There's a reason they don't drink that stuff and you just figured it out." Jack Henry laughed. "You know. There might be something to this payday thing and his leaving. The timing is off."

"Murdered," I corrected him. "So now you believe me?" The little confidence boost gave me the courage to take another swig.

"I believe evidence." Jack Henry stuck his hand up for the bartender to bring us another round.

"I told you. I told you." Cephus danced. "I was murdered by Vernon Baxter. Tell him it was Vernon."

I ignored Cephus and finished off the can of Stroh's. The bartender set another round down, along with our order of wings.

"Say, when was the last time you saw Cephus?" Jack Henry asked questions that started from the beginning. Questions I should have started with.

The bartender picked up the unopened Stroh's can and flipped it over to the bottom.

"Five years ago." He showed us the print on the bottom of the can. "I only bought Stroh's for Cephus and the expiration date shows five years ago."

"Yuck!" My face contorted. "No wonder it's

sour. I can't believe you gave me five-year-old beer."

"Hey"—he shrugged—"you asked for an ice-cold Stroh's." He laughed, walking down the bar and helping the other customers.

I grabbed Jack Henry's draft and took a drink.

"See. Five years ago he went missing. He had some sort of payday gone wrong. But what?" My mind reeled with possibilities. I continued while Jack Henry devoured the wings. "It had to be horse racing. Keeneland is right here. There is a bar there. He had to be gambling or something."

"Gambling." Jack Henry thought for a second. He licked his fingers. "I'll check into the files to see if there had been some sort of gambling joint around here five to ten years ago. That was before my police duties here."

"You are wasting your time." Cephus pouted. "I'm telling you, Vernon Baxter killed me."

Cephus was killing me. There was no tie to Vernon. *No stone unturned.* I would make a friendly visit to Vernon tomorrow, ask some questions and try to figure out what he knew about Leotta and Cephus Hardy.

Tonight, I was going to spend the rest of the night fulfilling my promise to Jack Henry. A night of romance.

Chapter 11

W hat the hell?" I launched myself to a sitting position in the bed, my heart pounding a million miles a second. "I have a gun!" I yelled into the dark.

I knew I should've taken Jack Henry up on his offer to spend the night. Every time I had stuck my nose where it didn't belong, Eternal Slumber had been broken into. And I couldn't help but wonder if someone from the Watering Hole had overheard my conversation with Jack Henry or the bartender had loose lips.

I flipped on the lamp on the bedside table to find Cephus standing over me. He got closer and took a nice long whiff of my head.

"Cephus Hardy! Are you the one who woke me

up?" I looked at the clock. "It's two in the morning. What is wrong with you?"

"I was getting a little whiff of the Stroh's on your breath." He waved his hand in front of his nose. "There is a little bad breath mixed in but I still got a good whiff." He smacked his lips together.

"Are you kidding me?" I threw myself back on my pillow and pulled the covers up to my chin. "It's late. Do you want me to go see Vernon Baxter in the morning or not?"

"Of course I want you to go see that murderous bastard," Cephus harrumphed.

"Then let me go to bed," I begged.

"Just one more teeny-tiny whiff." He put his fingers together in the universal "little bit" sign.

I took a good long inhale and slowly exhaled the stale beer out of my mouth toward him. He closed his eyes and smiled. I closed my eyes and, before I knew it, my alarm was sounding off.

"Ugh." I groaned, peeling away the strand of hair that had dried on the drool on my cheek. I rubbed my head. There was a nasty headache brewing and I was sure it was from the Stroh's. "Nasty beer."

I threw back the covers and took a nice long shower, happy to recall that my phone hadn't rung in the middle of the night as it frequently did since people loved to die then. Why was that?

Though we could use a client for business, I did need to get Cephus to the other side.

"What are we doing today?" Cephus asked.

I pulled my hair back into a ponytail and applied a little bit of lipstick as I looked in the small mirror that hung on the wall in the hallway.

"I told you at two in the morning," I said. "I'm going to talk to Vernon Baxter since he is finished with the autopsy and we don't have any clients. It would be a good time to go and just question him."

"I'm telling you. Take a look in that garden." His words eerily sent a cold rush all over my body.

I turned to look at him, but he was gone.

"You love leaving me hanging," I called out in the air, grabbed my cell from the wall charger and headed out the door.

Vernon Baxter lived on the opposite side of town from the Watering Hole.

A flash of Granny on her scooter zoomed past me or at least my peripheral vision thought so. Her flag wasn't there but I knew it was her though she didn't look back. As far as I knew, no one else in Sleepy Hollow had a moped. Granny hadn't either until she took her car to an auction in Lexington and came back with a scooter. I thought she had lost her marbles. She had gotten much better at driving it.

I slammed the brakes of the hearse when I brought my eyes from the rearview mirror to the front windshield. A goat darted out in front of me. A bunch of goats darted out in front of me.

"Damn goats." I beeped the horn at the herd as they jumped and ran.

It looked like Sanford Brumfield's goats had gotten out again and were headed straight for Dottie Kramer's house.

I grabbed my phone off the passenger seat and texted Jack Henry.

Looks like the goats are out again. You better get out here before Dottie Kramer gives you an earful.

I turned in to Vernon's at the next driveway. It was long and windy like the road getting here. Vernon's car was there. I pulled up next to it.

He had a nice little brick ranch with a good bit of property.

"Yeppers! He killed me right over there," Cephus chirped from the back of the hearse. He was getting very comfortable, sitting on the gurney.

I looked in the direction Cephus claimed was his place of death. There were visible markings of what used to be a garden. A small brick wall made a rectangle around the weeds and was crumbling to the ground. The weeds were overgrown and didn't look like they had been tended to in over five years. If there was a thriving garden under there, I would have been surprised.

Damn. I told him yesterday that if they got out one more time, I was going to have to fine him, Jack Henry had sent back.

Vernon stood on the front-porch slab of concrete with a cup of coffee in his hand so I didn't have time to text Jack Henry back. I really wanted to. I wanted to know if he had gotten any information about gambling or possible gambling rings in Sleepy Hollow.

"Emma Lee." Vernon nodded when I got out of the car. "What are you doing here?"

"I thought I'd come by and shoot the breeze." I pointed to the road. "Say, Granny wasn't by here, was she?"

I had to make sure that my mind wasn't playing games on me. Considering my special job as a Betweener, my mind was sometimes a bit foggy on what was real and what wasn't. She was on a mission to become mayor and she wasn't leaving early-daylight hours to chance.

"Come on in and grab a cup of coffee." He held the door open.

"Don't do it," Cephus warned. His eyes lowered, his lips pursed. "He is a murderer. I'm proof."

"I'd love a cup. Thanks." I walked in the house and stepped aside for him to pass me after he shut the door.

"Zula Fae did come by an hour or so ago. Said she was handing out material." He tapped a brochure and a button Granny had left. They were was sitting on the table in the entryway.

Vernon gestured for me to follow him. And I did.

"Some killer." I threw my head back to show Cephus that Vernon had left the front door open and the screen door was the only thing between me and freedom. "Killers don't leave doors wide open," I muttered under my breath.

"What was that?" Vernon stopped in the middle of his kitchen.

"Granny sure does want to win." I was pleasantly surprised at his bachelor pad. "Nice place."

The kitchen was decorated in brown cabinets. There was a large mahogany island in the center and at least eight barstools around it. There was no table or chairs so I moseyed up to the island and planted myself on a stool.

"Your coffee smells great." The scent of freshly pressed coffee beans hung around my nose.

Cephus moved around the room, taking in everything like he was the one doing the detective work.

When Vernon turned to retrieve the cream from the refrigerator, I gave Cephus my best mean face, pointed at him, and through gritted teeth, I silently warned, "Don't you lay a finger on him."

"Fine. You'll see." Cephus left just like he appeared. Into thin air.

"I know you like cream." Vernon put the cup of coffee and the creamer container in front of me. "I don't use a fancy creamer pot."

"Me neither." I grabbed the container and twisted the lid off, pouring some cream in the black cup of joe, creating a milky drink.

"So why are you here?" he asked.

"I wanted to make sure you had a button from Granny. She's been all over my ass about this election. She beat me to it." I smacked the island top. "Did she invite you to the meet-the-candidate cookout tonight?"

"No, she didn't." He took a drink. "I know the candidate. Maybe that's why."

"It's for the entire town and I'd love for you to be there." I lifted myself up by my toes on the stool's foot bar and planted my hands on the island. "You sure do have some lovely property."

"It's been nice to come out here and relax after work." He nodded.

"You retired early, right?" I was starting to lay the groundwork.

"I did." He looked out the window over his property. "Do you want to go see how far the property goes?"

"Sure," I said, and took my cup of coffee and walked out with him through the back door, which was in the kitchen. "Are those the mountains that are situated behind the Sleepy Hollow Inn?"

The land was beautiful. Breathtaking. His acres were rolling, and in the distance, you could see the mountains. Definitely not walkable distance, but it was nice to look at. Especially in the early morning like now, when the fog was still hanging over the peaks.

"It is." The steam rolled off his cup and around his head when he took a drink.

"What's that over there?" I asked, knowing what was in the weeded box.

I walked over to the overgrown garden.

"I used to have the best garden. That was another life."

Another life? I gulped.

"I loved coming home after a long day of seeing patients and working in the garden. Digging in the soil. Watching seedlings grow." There was pride in his voice. "I never even had to go to the grocery store for my vegetables. Fresh every night for dinner. Nothing I love better than a good plump tomato."

"It looks like you had a nice thing going." I kicked one of the broken bricks and took a look-see in the weeds. Surely to God, if Cephus was in there, his fancy white, patent-leather shoes would still be there. Maybe not his bones, but the shoes. Well, I guess a killer would get rid of the clothes and body. "Why don't you garden again?"

"Nah. It takes a couple of years to get some of the vegetables going." He cackled. "I might be dead by then." He held his hand out. "I need a refill. Do you want a topper?"

"Sure." I couldn't believe my luck.

I handed him the cup and when he was out of sight, I jumped feetfirst in the garden and swept my foot along the weeds, exposing the earth below. I hurried up and down the dirt and weeds, searching for anything. I had almost given up all hope when something caught my eye.

I bent down and noticed it was half-buried. I loosened the dirt around it and plucked it from the wet soil.

"Oh my God," I gasped and looked back when I heard the back door shut and Vernon walking back. "Cephus's ring."

"What are you doing?" Vernon had a perplexed look on his face. He steadied a hot cup of coffee in each hand.

I put the ring down and plucked a tiny tomato off the vine that was growing next to the ring.

"I saw this tomato. See, you can start your garden again." I put the tomato on a falling brick. "I gotta go."

"I thought you wanted a topper?" Vernon held out the cup.

"I didn't realize the time." I tapped the imaginary watch on my wrist. "See ya tonight!"

My heart was about to pound out of my chest. I tried to steady the hearse at a normal speed down Vernon Baxter's driveway and not let my nerves control my foot. My foot had other plans and the hearse gave in.

I shot the juice to it and zoomed right out of that driveway.

"Oh my God! I've got to call Jack Henry." I held on to the wheel with one hand and felt around the passenger seat for my phone with the other. "Jack!" I screamed with joy when I saw his Sleepy Hollow cruiser, lights flashing. He was corralling the goats with his baton in one hand and his other arm extended.

"What the hell?" Jack dropped his hands when the hearse came to a sliding halt.

It was all the goats needed to make a run for it, right across the street, up the hill, and into Dottie Kramer's garden.

"Shit," Jack Henry spat. He was so mad, his cheeks reddened. "You better have a good reason to come to a screeching stop."

"Jack . . ." I threw the door open and raced over to him. I gasped, "Vernon . . ." I bent over to try to catch my breath. My heart was pounding so hard and I was so scared, my nerves were tingling. I couldn't breathe. "Vernon Baxter murdered Cephus Hardy."

"Stand up. Take a breath." He encouraged me to calm down. "What is this nonsense about Vernon Baxter and murder? I thought we were looking at Terk Rhinehammer?"

"Don't be ridiculous," I quipped. "Cephus told me the last person he talked to was Vernon Baxter in Vernon's vegetable garden. Next thing he knew, he was dead. So I went over to see Vernon this morning, using Granny as an excuse and, long story short, got in the vegetable garden."

I pointed to my ring finger.

"Cephus Hardy always wore a gold ring with a large, square, black onyx in the middle. More onyx than gold. He never took it off." I took another deep breath. My nerves were starting to settle down. "I found the ring in the garden. Hand to God." I put my hand on my chest and made a crisscross.

"Are you sure?" he asked.

"I'm dead positive. It was the ring." I nodded.

"Jack Henry Ross!" Dottie Kramer ran out her front door with a hairnet on her head and waving a rolled-up newspaper. "If you don't get these damn goats out of my garden and arrest Sanford Brumfield, you're gonna have a killin' on your hands. Him and them damn goats. You hear me?" She shook the paper in the air and proceeded in her housecoat over to the garden, where she swatted at the goats.

Jack Henry threw his hands up in the air.

"I'm done with this. Please go tell Sanford to get over to Dottie Kramer's and round up those goats." He jumped in his squad car without even saying thank you or kissing me bye before he took off.

"Told ya he was a murderer." Cephus appeared with his hands behind his back and swayed. He was so proud.

"I still don't know why he would do it. What

was in it for him?" If he was going to say Leotta and those kids, I would have died right there and joined him.

"I don't know. Just know he did it." He followed me back to the hearse.

I put it in gear and made my way up Sanford Brumfield's driveway to find him hooking up the hitch of the trailer to his truck.

"I know, I know." Sanford muttered. "Don't you think that crazy broad has already called me? Hell, I can hear her screaming from across the way. She didn't need to use the phone."

"She's really mad." I shut the hearse door behind me and moseyed up to him. "Wouldn't you be mad if someone ruined years of hard gardening work in just a couple minutes. Goats can be disastrous."

"Don't you think I know that, Emma Lee. What are you? The undertaker or the Mr. Green Jeans?" He shook his head, still bent over, and looked at me. "I'm sorry. But I know someone is letting these goats out and I don't know who. But I will figure it out." He tapped his temple. "Mark my words."

"You need to make it right with Dottie Kramer first." I suggested, "What about a nice dinner out? That would be a good gesture, seeing she doesn't have much to eat now."

Sanford grumbled, then jumped in his truck.

"Bye now." I waved, hoping to get a smile, but there was nothing doing.

Sanford was on a mission to find out how those goats got out and I was on a mission to find out why Vernon Baxter would kill Cephus Hardy.

"Can we go now?" Cephus asked. "Head on back to the Watering Hole so you can have an ice-cold Stroh's and I can get a whiff?"

"What are you doing here?" I asked, and planted my hands on my hips.

"Whatcha mean?"

"I found your ring. And I'm sure Vernon is in custody. So . . ." I twirled my finger in a complete circle in front of him before I jutted it up to the sky. "Get going! And"—I pointed directly at him— "don't be telling anyone else about me. Ya hear?"

Cephus looked up. He stared long and hard, making all sorts of faces.

"What are you doing?" I asked.

"I'm trying to get up there, but nothin' is happenin'." He grunted a few more times and bore down like he needed to go to the bathroom. He stood back up. "See. Nothin'."

Chapter 12

hit, shit, shit!" I beat the wheel and hurried myself back to Vernon Baxter's. "I told you he didn't kill you. If he had, you wouldn't still be here."

I glanced in rearview, looking at Cephus as he contemplated my words.

"If he killed you, your murder would have been solved and you would have crossed over. Well, after you say good-bye to your loved ones you will cross over. But your feeling of being free will be felt when we figure out who murdered you."

"Oops." Cephus shrugged like we hadn't just ruined someone's day . . . life.

"Oops? Oops!" I screamed, and beat the steering wheel a couple more times until my palm hurt.

I was so mad, I wasn't sure how I was going to explain this one. "I should've never listened to a drunk."

"I . . . I . . ." Cephus disappeared.

"I'm sorry. I didn't mean that," I muttered into the air. "Sort of didn't mean it."

I did mean it. I knew that Vernon Baxter was no killer, no more than Granny . . .

Something snapped in my head. Images of the nasty breakfast food I thought she was going to feed the Inn's customers and thought maybe it wasn't for the Inn. I bet she was going to feed the goats. I bet she let the goats out and put that feed in Dottie Kramer's garden. That was why Granny was on this road.

"Hi, Granny," I said when she answered my phone call. I pulled back into Vernon Baxter's driveway so I could stop Jack Henry from arresting him. "How are you this morning?"

"I'm fine, dear." Granny was as nice as pie. "Did somebody kick the bucket?"

"No, why would you say that?" I asked.

I knew exactly why she would say that. Because she saw me this morning on the back road on my way here and didn't act like she saw me. The only real reason I would be on that road would be to pick up a client.

"You are up awfully early." Granny was good with her comebacks.

I got out of the hearse when I didn't see Jack Henry's squad car, but Vernon's car was there.

"I just wanted to call to make sure you didn't need anything for your Inn guests this morning." My own nicey-nice was making me sick. Granny taught me best. She'd say that honey catches more flies than vinegar, meaning, you can get what you want out of people by being nice and not pissy.

I knocked on Vernon's door.

"Cut the crap, Emma Lee, and getting all catty-wampus on me." Granny's tone turned. "You know and I know we saw each other this morning. What were you doing out on that foggy back road this morning?"

"I could ask you the same thing." I knocked louder and put my other ear to the door. There weren't any footsteps. I hooded my eyes with my free hand to see if I could see Vernon inside. My gut dropped. Jack Henry had taken him in. "Damn."

"Emma Lee Raines, what did I tell you about that cursing?" Granny was throwing a little bit of a hissy fit.

"Stop your conniption." I stomped back to the hearse. "I'm on my way over there to talk to you about why I think you were in the country, so you better get your story straight."

I hung up the phone before I could hear her tell me what was what. I knew what was what and I knew she would do anything to get a vote. Even if it was from Dottie Kramer.

I'm wrong about Vernon Baxter. I texted Jack Henry. *My friend is still here with me, which means nothing has been solved.*

Playing with someone's life isn't a joke. He texted back. Even his text tone gave me pause.

Jack Henry was mad. I could see him now, sitting across from Vernon Baxter asking all sorts of questions about a missing man that everyone believed had left on his own.

Unfortunately, there is probable cause with the ring. He has a warrant out for his arrest on past parking tickets from Lexington, so I'm keeping him for at least 24 hours. And he's lawyered up, Jack Henry sent. *I'll call you later.*

The text didn't sound like Vernon was a Boy Scout. He might not have murdered Cephus, but there was something there and maybe Cephus knew about that. Though I did recall Cephus telling me he had gone to see Vernon about Leotta. He used the term *knocking boots*. It wasn't a secret that Vernon Baxter had been an eligible bachelor since he lived in Sleepy Hollow. In fact, I would have fixed Granny up with him instead of Doc Clyde.

The carnival was completely set up when I passed on the back side of the square. I avoided driving around the square since it was prime breakfast time and I knew everyone would be out, walking to work or going to Higher Grounds to get a cup of coffee.

I parked the hearse in the lot across the street from the Inn. It was the square's parking lot and convenient so I didn't take up the guests' spots in the Inn's lot.

It was the same picture every morning. The rocking chairs were occupied. Each guest had a cup of coffee and rocked back and forth talking, with the other guests. The fog had burned off, the sky was baby blue, making it a great day to walk around the first day of the carnival or hike to the caves. It was a beautiful time of the year and busy for everyone.

"Good morning," I greeted an Inn guest on my way in through the screen door.

The room on the right was filled with more guests, who were either waiting for a table for breakfast or enjoying the continental breakfast goodies from Higher Grounds.

"Granny?" I pushed the door to the kitchen open.

Granny's normal flaming red hair was doused in flour. She held a bowl in the crock of her elbow and was viciously stirring with her other.

"I'm busy. Can't you see that?" Granny was in no mood for me to question her.

"Tell me." I saw the same bowl on the counter that had that strange berry mix. There was a piece of tin foil covering it. "Did you put the mixture in Dottie's garden first for Sanford's goats to find after you opened their gate? Or did you open the gate and tempt them over to Dottie's garden?"

"Now." Granny put her hand with the spoon covered with batter mix on her hip. It dripped on the floor. "I know how this politicking stuff works. I didn't just fall off the turnip truck. A vote is a vote."

"And Sanford is voting for you." I reminded her of his loyalty. "You are causing him to get fined and make an enemy out of his own neighbor."

"Dottie Kramer thinks she's all highfalutin out there with her little vegetable garden and going around telling everybody she's voting for O'Dell Burns." Granny started stirring again. This time a little faster. Her words flew, "I've got to beat O'Dell Burns. And every vote counts."

"But why are you having the goats eat her garden? That makes no sense." I took the foil off the bowl and looked in. "Yuck." My face contorted.

"Put that back on." Granny shook the spoon at me and went back to mixing. "The less you and that nosy sheriff boyfriend of yours know, the better off I am."

She set the bowl and spoon on the counter and walked over to me. She leaned in, her nose almost touching mine, her eyes squinting.

"Do you hear me, Emma Lee?" She growled, "Stay out of it. You never saw a thing. You don't know a thing. You ain't too old for me to jerk a knot in you."

"Okay. But don't come calling me when they figure out it was you and put you in jail right next to Vernon Baxter." I slammed my mouth shut when Vernon's name spewed out of my mouth.

"Vernon Baxter is in jail?" Granny jumped back. "He has the personality of a dishrag. What did he do? Use too much embalming fluid?"

"Nothing. He did nothing." I could kick my own butt for letting that slip out.

Granny was my granny, but Granny was still a gossip, just like every other breathing, breasted woman in Sleepy Hollow.

"We'll see about that. I bet Beulah knows about

that." Granny flung her hands up in the air, sucked in a big breath, and bent down to the floor, doing her best to touch her toes. "I'm a bit stressed. I think I need to make that early yoga class over at Hettie's new place."

"I don't think you do, Granny." I shook my head. I knew what was going to come out of her mouth next.

"You don't mind." She untied her apron and handed it to me. "You don't have any funerals to tend to. It'll only be an hour or so."

She milled about, grabbing her purse, then the moped keys off the hook by the door.

"I don't think so, Granny." I put the apron on the kitchen table and tried to stop her.

"You are such a good granddaughter." She squeezed my cheeks together. "I have always been a little more partial toward you."

"Granny, you can't do this. You can't make those sorts of statements and make me feel better." I stomped my foot on the floor and watched the kitchen door swing back and forth when Granny darted out and didn't look back.

Chapter 13

The rush crowd was almost over when Granny up and left me in charge to go find out the gossip around town at Pose and Relax while taking the morning yoga class. Most of the Auxiliary women were in the early class so they could get on with their day and spread the gossip love.

After the last guest table was cleared and cleaned, I stuck a sign on the door that said breakfast hours in the dining room were over and they could go into the snack room off the hallway for the free muffins and coffee.

Even though Granny owned and operated the Inn, she didn't have to be there twenty-four/seven. She just needed to be there for the mealtimes since she was the chef. I had tried to get her to hire someone. She claimed no one made a better Southern, home-cooked meal than her. I wasn't going to argue with that.

This time I walked around the square and headed into Higher Grounds. It was still early and the only coffee I'd had was from Vernon Baxter. Poor Vernon. He was not far from my mind. I was having a hard time forgiving myself for accusing him of killing Cephus Hardy, though it was strange that I had found Cephus's ring in the garden where he claimed he was killed.

"She sure is purty." Cephus appeared next to me in line.

Ahem. I cleared my throat and looked ahead of me, where Mary Anna was talking with her hands, explaining some big beauty tip to Cheryl Lynne.

"Good morning, ladies." I smiled and butted my way into the conversation. "I hope to see both of you at Granny's meet-the-candidate cookout tonight."

"Of course I'm going to be there," Mary Anna confirmed. "Zula Fae is even letting me fix her hair. I swear that cap she wears when she's riding her fancy little bicycle is ruining the roots of her gorgeous hair. I told her she needed to put extra conditioning on, but you know Zula." Mary Anna shook her hair. It was styled in the classic Marilyn bob. I had no idea how she could breathe in the tight white dress. Her boobs toppled over the scalloped edges.

Looking at her feet in the sky-high heels made me cringe.

"And I'm doing the desserts. Well," Cheryl Lynne leaned in. Her long blond hair spilled over her shoulders. She would look good in a paper sack. Her perfect size six wore a little sundress and her apron was tied neatly around her waist, making it look even smaller.

She said, "Zula herself bought the carrots from Dottie Kramer for me to make the carrot cake."

"What?" I was taken aback. Granny never mentioned once about the carrots and her deal with Dottie Kramer. Had I been wrong about Granny and the goats? She never admitted it, but she never denied it either.

"She sure did. Dottie Kramer told me herself." Cheryl's brows lifted and my mouth and Mary Anna's mouth dropped.

"Honey, I've got to get going. Can you get me a cup to go?" Mary Anna asked Cheryl Lynne.

"Me too," I spoke up.

Eternal Slumber was right next door to Girl's Best Friend Spa. The walk would do me good. And I could pick Mary Anna's brain.

"See y'all tonight," Cheryl called after us on our way out.

"I wouldn't put anything past Zula Fae." Mary Anna cackled. She glanced over at me. "You need a touch-up."

"I do." I ran my hand along my ponytail. "Just make me an appointment and let me know."

That's the way we did things around here. She'd call me with a time and I'd make sure I was there. Life was slow in Sleepy Hollow, except when I was worried about getting someone to cross over. Which reminded me of Cephus.

"I saw your momma and Teddy," I said to start the conversation. "I can't believe the success Teddy has had."

"He's doing good for himself, especially since Daddy left." She kept her head forward. Her heels clicked like a horse's.

"You still haven't heard from him?" I asked.

"Not a word." She sighed deeply. "It's been five years ago almost to the day. Teddy and I were thinking about hiring a private investigator to follow up on some leads."

"What kinds of leads?" I asked.

"There have been a few sightings reported in Lexington at a few beer joints. And then there's the whole . . ." She paused. Her eyes filled with water. "You know." She hesitated. "Woman thing."

"Woman thing?" Of course I had heard, but I wasn't going to tell her.

"I never saw it, but I had heard that Daddy was a little bit of a womanizer." Her words were broken. "And what if an angry husband or boyfriend hurt Daddy. And"—her voice cracked— "he didn't make it out alive."

"Womanizer?" Cephus scratched his head. "I might be a lot of things, but I never cheated on Leotta. Mind you, I had plenty of opportunities. But I didn't do no such thing." He put his hand out like he had stuck it on a Bible in a court of law.

"I've never heard such a thing." I wanted to reiterate Cephus's claim of fidelity. "Did you hear that from them old banty hens?" I asked, and peered in the window of Pose and Relax.

They were in some sort of back-bend pose. How on earth that was relaxing was beyond me.

"Oh my." Mary Anna laughed and we stopped. "I've done walked clear past the shop."

"It's good catching up on girl talk." I put my hands on each side of her arms. "Your daddy loved your momma. Don't let anyone ever tell you different."

Those were the only encouraging words I could give her. I wished I could say, oh, he's fine, he'll turn up. He had turned up. As a ghost.

"Thank you, Emma Lee." Cephus stood on the sidewalk, watching Mary Anna walk back down the block and across the street to Girl's Best Friend Spa. "Thank you for making my baby feel better."

"You're welcome," I muttered under my breath, as my phone rang.

I pressed the TALK button and covered the phone with my hand as I answered.

"Jack Henry, I'm so sorry about the mislead. Cephus was sure of it," I whispered.

"Don't worry about it. When I ran Vernon's name, it came up he had a warrant so he thinks I've taken him in for that. When I took a look around his yard, I just happened upon the ring, thanks to you." Jack Henry was good using his instincts. "When I asked him about the ring, his face dropped. He told me it was Cephus Hardy's and he told me about the scuffle, only he said that when he came back out after taking a phone call, Cephus was gone."

"Did he say exactly what happened between them?" I asked, keeping my words vague.

People were everywhere. They were already

getting things going at the carnival and people from the neighboring towns were pouring in, along with the tourists.

"That's when he lawyered up on me. Some guy from Lexington," Jack Henry said. "I do have some news about the gambling thing I told you I would look into."

"Oh, yeah?" I made my way around Granny's blinking sign in Eternal Slumber's yard and up the steps of the funeral home.

I opened the door. It was eerily quiet, kind of like it was the calm before the storm. There was something in the air letting me know to hold on. Things were about to go down.

"Evidently, there was a newspaper in town. Due to poor sales and the growth in the Internet, the town council did away with the paper," he said.

I tried to recall the paper, but nothing was coming to me. It wasn't like I was clambering to read any sort of news in Sleepy Hollow a few years ago when I could just sit at Higher Grounds and overhear everything that was going on.

"Okay, what does that have to do with Cephus?"

I ducked into my office and shut the door behind me. When I had passed Charlotte's office, I heard her talking and her door was shut, which meant she was with a client. Maybe they wanted to do pre-need arrangements. We had a lot of those appointments.

"I found a report from years ago where Dottie Kramer had made a complaint that someone was running a gambling ring. The editor of the newspaper got ahold of it right before the city shut the paper down." He took a breath. I could hear paper shuffling in the background. "The story died along with the paper. It wasn't so long ago the paper was in town. Do you remember a paper in Sleepy Hollow?"

"Like we cared about the news." I reminded him that we were off at college having a good time, not worried about what was going on in Sleepy Hollow. "You said Dottie Kramer made the complaint?" I wondered what Dottie knew about a gambling ring. "Do you know the editor's name?"

"No. Like I said, it was years ago that the report was filed, which means it was before I got here." He paused. "I'm only telling you this because nothing is going on around here. I believe Cephus is dead and his ring is a strange thing, but you don't need to stick your head where there might be danger. Please leave it to me."

"Okay." My mind reeled about this editor and the story that had been about to break.

"I'm serious," Jack Henry warned me.

He knew as well as I that I wasn't going to just let that die.

"It's easy for you to say." I yawned. "You aren't the one who is getting woken up in the middle of the night getting sniffed."

"W-what?" Jack Henry asked.

"Nothing." I didn't have time to explain anything to him. I had to get to the courthouse so I could look at the past records of a newspaper and gather a name of a certain editor. "I'll see you at Granny's meet-the-candidate cookout?"

"I'll be there."

We hung up the phone. I left my office and walked down the hall to Charlotte's office. She was still going over the packages with the client and I continued out the door.

Chapter 14

V ote O'Dell for Mayor." Bea Allen's voice projected through the megaphone, spilling out into the street right in front of the courthouse and the carnival. "O'Dell Burns for Mayor."

"Where's the candidate?" I asked, walking up to her, Leotta and Teddy.

"He's busy. There is a funeral service taking place in a couple hours." There was a smug look on her face. "What about Eternal Slumber? You busy?"

"We are. In fact, Charlotte is talking with clients right now while I do some research." I gestured to the courthouse.

"Teddy, how long you in town?" I wanted to change the subject.

"I'm cutting the ribbon for the ceremony tonight at the gazebo." He smiled. "Who would've thought that I would be back here cutting any ribbon."

"I think it's great." I wasn't sure whether now was the time or place to ask about his dad's gambling. I tugged his shirt and pulled him to the side. "I hate to be nosy, but with you back and Mary Anna working for me, we talk about your dad all the time," I lied, "and she's still so upset about how he just upped and left."

"Yeah"—a long sigh escaped him—"Mary Anna has taken it real hard. Sometimes I wish she'd just move out of this town so she can move on, but she thinks she needs to be here just in case Dad comes back."

"Your dad was so good to you and your family. It just seems so weird that he would disappear without telling you." I shook my head in shame.

"I was about to go to the state wrestling match too." Teddy's jaw clenched. The sun bounced off his bald head. "I was so mad at him for not showing up. I figured he was on a binge." His biceps tensed. I noticed he was fisting his hands.

"Do you know anything about a gambling ring he might have been associated with?" I asked nonchalantly.

"Gambling? Dad would never waste his money on gambling. He drank every dollar he earned. It's a shame. I wish he could see me now." Teddy looked out over the square as though he was thinking about his dad and what could've been.

"I wish there was something I could do for Mary Anna." I didn't want to continue asking questions. I could see the pain in him. "She's such a great employee. And she can't leave town." I ran my hand over my hair. "Who'd fancy me up for my dates with Jack Henry?"

"Wait." A sneaky grin crossed Teddy's lips. "You and Jack Henry Ross are an item?"

"Ye-es." I dropped my mouth for a dramatic effect. "Why?"

"The creepy funeral-home girl and the jock? And I thought I'd seen it all since I've traveled the world." Jokingly, he nudged me.

"Funny." I rolled my eyes.

Ahem. Bea Allen cleared her throat and raised her drawn-on brows sky-high and tapped that big, ugly toe. She pumped her election sign up and down, gesturing Teddy to do the same.

"If you would please excuse me." I pushed my way around Bea Allen and her small army carrying the VOTE FOR O'DELL signs. "I'll see you tonight, Teddy."

I hurried up the concrete steps and pushed the heavy glass doors open into the old marble hallway. Doors ran along the entire hallway and above each door hung a small sign. I was looking for the Record Room and on the way there I just happened to peek in the mayor's office and pictured Granny sitting at the large desk in front of the large window that overlooked Sleepy Hollow.

Granny would make a good mayor because she was relentless and would get things done.

"How can I help you?" The deputy clerk stood up from behind the tall counter and blew a breath of air, causing her bangs to fly upward. "It's hot in here."

"It sure is." I fanned myself with my hand like it was really going to create a difference. "Hey, do you know anything about a newspaper that used to be in Sleepy Hollow?"

"Hmm . . ." Her lips twisted around, she tapped her temple with her finger. She brought the finger toward me and shook it. "You know"—she paused and looked up in the air—"I recall someone saying something about a newspaper, but I don't think it was long-lived. Most people get their news or put their news in the Lexington paper."

"Right." I snapped my fingers. "I'm looking for the paper that was here."

"Let me ask Viola. She's been here as long as the courthouse." The deputy clerk winked. She put the back of her hand up to cover her mouth. "Not really, but you know what I mean."

I laughed to make her feel better. I didn't care how old Viola was, I wanted the information I asked about.

The deputy clerk was only gone for a minute when she came back with a piece of paper.

"Viola said there was a paper here a while ago and short-lived. There was only one person that ran it. She couldn't recall the name, but she did say the paper was located at the old mill." She slid the paper across the counter toward me.

There was some sort of address scribbled on it. It had to be the old-mill address. I already knew where it was, but I took the piece of paper anyway and thanked her for her time.

Armed with the knowledge that Bea Allen and her little army of electioneers were in front of the courthouse, I slipped out the side door and made my way back to the hearse, which was still parked in the lot across from the Inn.

I wanted to drive out to the mill and see if there was any evidence of the paper. If I could get the name of the editor, I might be able to track him down and see exactly what he knew.

"Where we going?" Cephus sat in the passenger seat of the hearse.

"We are going to the old mill to see if I can track down an editor from the old newspaper from here. He had a tip on a gambling ring around here." I took the piece of paper that Terk Rhinehammer had out of my pocket and held it up for Cephus to see.

He squinted. He fidgeted. And he huffed.

"Do you want to tell me about what you are feeling?" I asked. "And not do the old disappearing act like you have been doing."

He sighed so big, his shoulders heaved up and fell down.

"If you really want to go to the other side, and you really want me to help figure out who murdered you, I have to know you inside and out. Your life. Your drinking. Your womanizing. And your gambling habits."

"Hey now, I told you I was faithful to Leotta. Can't say she was, but I was." He beat his chest like a gorilla. "The gambling might be another story. Something I'm not proud of."

"Did you bet on the ponies?" It was so easy for everyone to run up to Lexington and place bets at the Keeneland Racetrack.

"Something like that." His lips clamped down. "If Teddy knew, he'd be so disappointed. I can't even imagine what Mary Anna would think." He was silent for a few seconds. "Do you think someone killed me over a gambling deal?"

"Maybe. Money does strange things to people." I eased the hearse up to the old mill and put it in PARK. "Did you owe money to someone?"

"No. I was a winner. Natural." Pride spewed out of his eyes. "I made a lot of money that way."

"Can you tell me who was in the gambling ring?" I asked.

"I don't know. It was all done on the down-low. I would leave a piece of paper with what I wanted to bet on and it was done. I would go to the same spot and pick up my winnings. Granted, I went directly to the Watering Hole to celebrate."

"The bartender from there told me you were waiting on a big payday."

"Big payday?" he questioned. "One thing about this ghost thing, your memory isn't always as clear as if I were living."

"Hence Vernon Baxter?" I was still feeling guilty.

I thought of Vernon Baxter sitting in the tiny cell at the Sleepy Hollow jail. He was probably alone unless Jack Henry had pulled someone over coming through town after leaving the Watering Hole. Most of the time, the residents of the jail were the drunk drivers needing to sober up.

"I'm sorry I accused him of killing me, but I'm not sorry for the sack of crap he is. Maybe sitting in the jail will give him time to think back about how he tried to break up me and Leotta." Anger spewed from his mouth.

"Cephus." The old mill was not in the best shape. There were more clapboards hanging off the side than hammered in. "You are going to have to get over that. I hate to tell you that you're dead. Don't you want Leotta to be happy?"

"No one made Leotta happy but me." He crossed his arms and lifted his chin in a debonair way.

"When you were living. What about now?" I asked. "Don't you want her to be with someone like Vernon Baxter, who can give her anything?"

"You sayin' I didn't give her anything? I did." His brows furrowed. "I took her to the flea market every single weekend, giving her twenty-five dollars, telling her she could get whatever she wanted. If that ain't treatin' a woman right, then I don't know what was."

"How generous of you," I said in a monotone voice.

"Besides, she's with Terk Rhinehammer." Nervously, he tapped the windowsill. "That makes me mad too. Why are we here?"

"I need to find the editor of the old Sleepy Hollow newspaper." I opened the door and got out.

I put my hands on my hips and took a good look around me. I wasn't sure what the best way to get into the mill was going to be. The large, wooden, sliding door had ivy grown up and around it. There was no way in there unless I had cutters to cut the vine.

"I thought you were working on my case?" he muttered. "I knew Chicken Teater was crazy when he was alive. Seems like dying didn't help him any. He gave bad advice."

I took a deep breath. There was no sense in arguing with a ghost. I took the first steps toward the mill and noticed another small door on the side that was hanging off the top hinges. The weeds around it had grown up and kept it open.

I grabbed the emergency kit out of the back of the hearse and took out the flashlight.

I pointed the flashlight through the open door into complete darkness. With the help of the light, I could see there was a desk and some papers scattered around. That was my target. With the flashlight aimed on the prize, I slipped into the mill, letting the darkness wrap around me.

Prickles traveled up my legs and arms. I knew I wasn't in any harm, but the thought of a creepy mill and the darkness reminded me of one of those scary movies that I would see on the TV and scream at the girl to walk back up the stairs and not go down into the dark basement, where the killer was waiting for her.

"Cephus?" I asked.

Not that he was going to be able to help me if a killer was in there, but knowing he was there did make me feel better.

"No way I'm going in there," Cephus called out from behind me. "I don't like snakes."

"Me either, but you need me to figure out who killed you, right?" I asked, and took another step.

Something scurried around my foot and I immediately flashed the light to the ground.

"Oh my God!" I screamed when the rat ran in the opposite direction. "Hurry, hurry." I encouraged myself to see what was on the table.

There were all sorts of notes and notebooks, along with a copy of the newspaper. I flashed the light to the top of it. The volume number was nine and the notepad next to it said volume ten.

"You see something?" Cephus asked from the outside.

"I think the paper ran nine weeks because of

the volume numbers." I glanced down at the note-book and saw the words *gambling ring* printed on it. "I think I found something."

Just as I grabbed the paper, some sort of explosion happened, knocking me to the ground.

"Emma Lee?" I heard Cephus call out my name through the dust. "Emma Lee?" His voice was a little more frantic this time.

"Over here!" I coughed out, and tried to sit up. The papers were still in my grip.

"Get out!" Cephus was more urgent than ever. "Or you'll be joining me on this side!"

I jumped up and tried to run as fast as I could to the small light from the outside world coming through the door. I could see Cephus's outline.

"What?" My head hurt. The smell of fire made my head twirl around.

Flames fluttered around the old mill's ceiling right before another explosion blew the roof off.

"Hurry!" He motioned with his hands. The look on his face told me I better haul ass. "Hurry!" Urgency rang in my ears.

I flung myself out the door and outside the mill and landed on the ground just in time. The mill shot up to the sky, exploding into pieces.

Chapter 15

I scrambled away on my knees and hands, still gripping the papers, and planted my body up against the hearse. The sound of sirens echoed in the background.

"Emma Lee, are you okay?" Cephus stood next to me, the look of concern set deep in his eyes.

I nodded, taking in several breaths. My chest heaved up and down. Fire engines roared up the road. I opened the hearse door and threw the papers inside. I tried to steady my shaking hands when I saw the fire trucks pull in and Jack Henry closely following them in his cop car.

"Emma Lee?" Jack Henry jumped out of the cruiser and rushed to my side.

Immediately, I started to cry. A lump caught in my throat. It was the closest to death I had ever come. And I wasn't ready to join my clients on the other side.

I melted into Jack Henry's arms. He rubbed and kissed my head, letting me know it was going to be all right.

"What are you doing here?" he asked.

The firefighters were busy trying to put out the flames from the burning mill. Black smoke billowed around us.

Jack Henry ushered me back to his car. He took a blanket out from the trunk and placed it over me once he got inside next to me.

"Please don't tell me this has to do with Cephus Hardy." He already knew the answer before I had to admit to it. "Damn, Emma Lee. I almost lost you."

"I'm fine." I shook off the notion that I really did almost go up in flames.

"I don't care. What about the next time you get a hair up your butt and decide to investigate?" He rolled down his window when the fire inspector walked over and gestured for him to roll it down.

"I can tell you right now that this was no accident." He held a piece of pipe in his hands along with some wire nuts. "Someone wanted this place to no longer exist. I'll finish up after they get all the flames out, but this was found a few feet from the back."

"I'll be right back." Jack Henry got out of the car and walked behind where the old mill used to sit.

He squatted and looked around the tall grass. I watched as he got up and looked through it. There was nothing behind the old mill but a creek and woods.

"Someone knew you were here." Cephus played with the ring on his finger. "They knew you were here and wanted to make sure whatever it was that was in there stayed there."

"Right." My head felt like someone had taken a hammer to it. "Or they were sending me a clear warning to stop nosing around."

Patiently, I waited in the car for Jack Henry to finish up the quick investigative work before he drove me home and tucked me in the bed.

One thing I loved about my small town was no matter what your relationship was with someone, in the time of tragedy, everyone pulled together.

Word had spread fast about the old-mill explosion. Everyone and their brother had called to make sure I was okay and if there was anything they could do for me. Even Beulah Paige Bellefry stopped by with some lemon bars.

"I'm fine," I assured Granny from the comfort of my bed. "I promise. I don't need to see Doc Clyde."

Granny wasn't happy with my answer but hung up anyway.

"I'm ordering you to stop looking into Cephus's death." Jack Henry sat on the edge of my bed. "I swear I will lock you up in the cell with Vernon Baxter if you don't. That way I'll know that you are safe."

"I'm fine." I bit my lip. I had yet to see what the papers I had confiscated said. "Where is my car?"

"I had one of the firefighters drive it back." He rubbed his hand along my face. "I don't know what I would have done if you were in there during the explosion."

He bent down and gently kissed my lips. I put my hand behind his neck to keep him there. His kisses were better than any headache medicine.

"I'm fine," I assured him again when he pulled away.

"Can you remember what happened?" Jack Henry pulled out a notebook from the pocket of his cop shirt.

"Really?" I asked.

"Someone wanted that place gone. And I can't help but have a feeling that someone knew you were out there." He tapped the pad with his pencil. "I'm not going to let them get away with it."

I flung the covers back and swung my feet around to the floor to sit next to him.

"All I know is that I went to the mill to see if I could see any remains of the newspaper." I rubbed his leg, hoping it would help him forget some of the questions he was about to barrage me with.

It didn't work. He stood up and paced back and forth, drilling me.

"Why?"

"Because I can't help but think Cephus was somehow in that gambling ring. I want to talk to the editor."

"Did you make it inside the mill?"

"Yes."

"Did you see anything?" he asked, his eyes focused on me as though I were in the interrogation room.

"Nope. Not a thing." I pressed my lips together in a frown. "I walked out, and the next thing I knew, there was an explosion."

"You weren't inside when it exploded?" he asked.

I shook my head.

"Hmm." He wrote on the pad. "The explosion was from a few pipe bombs. One would have destroyed it, but two would destroy any contents, including you."

"I get it." I threw my hands in the air. The clock said it was about time for Granny's meet-the-candidate grill out. "I'm starving."

I steadied myself on the bed and stood up.

"Where do you think you are going?" He rushed to my side.

"I'm not going to let someone scare me. I'm going to Granny's event." I walked into the bathroom and turned the faucet on.

"Emma Lee, I don't like this one bit." He followed my every move. "I'm calling a deputy to come in so I can stay by your side. At least until I can get some answers back from the fire marshal."

I grinned ear to ear. "If I'd known a little explosion would help us spend more time together, I'd have put myself in danger a long time ago." I batted my lashes before I headed into the shower.

Tonight, I would be a good girl, but tomorrow was a different story. I had the article the editor was working on and I hoped there was a name or a clue for me to look into. Yes, tonight I would be the good granddaughter and girlfriend. But tomorrow . . . I would follow up any leads. No one was going to try to kill me and get away with it.

It was personal now.

Chapter 16

'm fine," I assured everyone who asked me during Granny's meet-the-candidate affair.

Granny was busy handing out flags and buttons. Jack Henry never left my side. Even Hettie Bell gave me some yoga moves to help with my sore body.

"I still don't know why you were out there." Disappointment settled in Charlotte Rae's deep hazel eyes.

She wasn't buying the whole story that I was just taking a drive.

"I'm glad you are here." I changed the subject. "Granny appreciates it."

"Ummhmm." She gave me the wonky eye and brought the glass of tea up to her lips.

"I'm going to grab a pulled-pork sandwich. Do you want one?" I asked before I scurried away.

Even if she did want one, I wasn't going to return to talk to her. Charlotte Rae had good instincts and she knew when I was lying. Jack Henry and I had agreed to the story I was telling everyone.

If there was someone trying to kill me or scare me off the gambling track, we didn't want them to try again.

"How's she doing?" Mary Anna walked up and pointed to Granny.

"Hey!" I was thrilled to see Mary Anna, Leotta and Teddy standing there. "I'm so glad you are here."

"I'm not saying I'm voting for Zula." Leotta wanted to make it clear. "I'm just here to see what all the candidates have to say. Bea Allen has been my best friend for years and I'm trying to spend time with her while she's here."

Leotta tucked her arm into the crook of Teddy's elbow.

"Plus Teddy and Mary Anna wanted to come support her since she's doing everything she can for O'Dell's campaign." Leotta smiled.

Cephus appeared next to her. It was the first time I had seen him since the accident at the mill this afternoon. He was so proud, looking at his family. There were tears in his eyes, making my eyes tear up.

Leotta reached out and grabbed my hand.

"We heard about the accident at the old mill." She squeezed my hand. "I'm so glad you weren't hurt."

"That's terrible." Teddy shook his head. "Do they know what happened?"

"Not that I know of." I shrugged. "I was on my way to a pre-need funeral arrangement appointment and I had forgotten about that old mill. When I saw it, I decided to pull over and look at it."

"Oh my God, Emma Lee." Mary Anna's eyes popped. "Were you inside when it exploded?"

"No." I was getting good at this lying stuff. "I was by my car and the next thing I knew, pow!" I threw my hands in the air, gesturing an explosion.

"Can I have your attention?" Granny's voice boomed over the crowd that had come to see her.

The carnival music and kids' screaming from the rides were in the background.

"I wanted to take the time to thank everyone for coming out tonight." She did a good job of looking around the crowd as she talked. "I made all sorts of goodies for you and some of my sweet tea, so be sure to grab something before you go over to the carnival."

Dottie Kramer stood near the tree. I was surprised to see her there. We all knew she was for O'Dell Burns. Sanford Brumfield wasn't too far away from her though you could tell they were keeping their distance.

"Emma Lee, I wanted to talk to you before you leave tonight." Leotta's face was serious. The lines around her eyes deepened.

I wasn't sure, but it looked like she knew something important and wanted to tell me, but right now wasn't the time.

"Okay," I said before the three of them walked off.

"What is that about?" Cephus asked.

"I don't know," I whispered. I glanced over at Jack Henry, who had been talking to some of the citizens who were inquisitive about the explosion. "I don't know."

Leotta knew something and she wanted me to know. I made a mental note to be sure to talk to her before the night was over.

"Tonight, I'm excited that Teddy Hardy has come to town to be our official ribbon cutter for the carnival fun." Granny pointed to Teddy, who raised his hand to the crowd. "A true star."

Teddy's face turned a bright red, like the color of Granny's hair.

"Before Teddy comes up here to cut the ribbon, I'd like to ask you for your vote. You let me take care of your loved ones when they moved beyond the physical world. I'm asking you to let me take care of you." Granny smiled and raised her hands in the air.

The crowd applauded and started to chant *Zula Fae*.

"Lordy." Charlotte Rae walked up and leaned in. "Just one more thing to make her head even bigger."

"Stop it." I laughed. Charlotte was right. Granny loved the attention.

The rally went on for a few more minutes. Teddy took the big scissors and was surrounded by the town-council members. He cut the ribbon. Everyone went crazy.

Some small children had photos of Teddy in his wrestling uniforms and had him autograph them, along with some posters. Leotta, Mary Anna and Cephus beamed as they watched our local celebrity.

There was a little pride in all of us. As far as I knew, there weren't any other celebrities who had come out of Sleepy Hollow. It was kind of exciting.

"You ready for that elephant ear?" Jack Henry asked.

"You bet." I entwined my fingers in his and let him lead the way. "I've been watching them set this thing up over the past couple of days, craving the fattening things."

The carnival was in full swing. Lines for the tilt-a-whirl and the Ferris wheel are always long. The zero-gravity ride, where you stand up, that twirled around and around, sideways and backward, made me sick just watching it.

"Anyone wanna go faster?" the carnie screamed in the microphone at the Himalayan ride. "Screeeeeammmm!"

The riders erupted in screams. The carnie did what he said he was going to do and shot the juice to the Himalayan, sending the ride faster and faster around the track.

Jack Henry and I laughed. Everyone was having a good time and I had even forgotten about my unfortunate run-in with a pipe bomb this afternoon.

"You better go save Zula Fae." Cheryl Lynne nodded toward the dunking tank.

The clown was on the small seat, dangling over the water. His feet barely skimmed the water level. Granny had her fist in the air, her mouth going a mile a minute. O'Dell Burns and Bea Allen Burns were laughing hysterically next to her.

"Oh no." My eyes grew big and I glanced over at Jack Henry before I darted off in Granny's direction.

"Knock me in the water, water," the clown taunted Granny. His voice rang over the crowd from a speaker on a tripod stand. "Come on, old lady, knock me in the waaaater, water!"

Granny grabbed a ball from bucket at her feet and threw it at the target as hard as she could. I could see the anger written all over her face. I wasn't sure if she was mad at his taunting her or calling her old.

"Waaaa." The clown put his hands up to his eyes like a crying baby. "You can't knock a clown in the water. How are you going to run a town?"

"It's on!" Granny yelled, and grabbed a ball for each hand.

She turned her body to the side, lifted her leg, and did a windup of her arm. The ball whizzed through the air, missing. A second time. Missed again.

"Waaaaa! I wouldn't vote for you!" He pointed and laughed at Granny. He put his hand up to his ear like a telephone. "Hello, nursing home. We have a live one. Come get her!"

"That sonofa . . ." Granny started, but I interrupted her.

"Granny." I grabbed her arm, and whispered, "Stop this. People are looking at you. It's a stupid clown trying to get your goat."

I kicked the bucket of balls out of her way and looked up at the clown. His eyes were haunting. His grin was evil.

"You should be ashamed of yourself!" I jutted my not-so-nice, ladylike finger toward him.

I probably shouldn't have done it, and it wasn't a good-Southern-girl thing to do. But as we all know—in the South, do not mess with my granny.

"Aw, Emma Lee, I was just playing around." The clown's makeup made his frown even more frown-y. He pointed to his outfit. "Part of the job. What about that beer?"

"Ugh. Digger Spears, I'm telling your momma when I see her!" I warned, and stormed off to find Granny.

"Wait. Digger Spears?" Jack Henry tried to keep up with me. "Beer? What did that clown mean by beer?" Jack sidestepped. "Is that clown Digger Spears, and did he ask you out on a date?"

"Yes and sort of." I didn't want to get into it with Jack Henry about it.

"Did you tell him that we were an item?" He grabbed my arm and stopped me in my tracks.

"No. I didn't." I jerked away. "I was too busy trying to get over to the Inn to help Granny. He was nice enough to say hello and tell me about the carnival and his life dreams." It struck me that Jack Henry was jealous. And it was kind of cute. I had never pictured Jack Henry being jealous of anyone with me. "If I'd known you were going to react like this, I might have told you."

"Oh stop it." His dimples deepened. "I love you and that clown was out of line asking you for a beer while he was working."

"It's Digger Spears. He's harmless. I've got to go to Granny." I pointed to the Auxiliary women who were over at Granny's side of the carnival shouting about voting for Granny.

"Need an ice-cold Stroh's, Teddy?" Digger Spears asked over the small microphone, ending with a cackle.

Teddy waved him off. It was just enough to keep Digger going.

"Big bad Teddy is going to get me in a headlock and give me a noogie. Wooooo . . ." Digger stuck his hands out in front of him. "I'm so scared." Digger stood up on the little diving board and made some muscle-building poses with his skinny arms.

Teddy grabbed a ball and flung it toward the target, missing by a mile.

"Hee, hee." Teddy plopped back down on his butt. A crowd had really started to gather to hear the funny clown. "Knock me in the waaaater, water!"

Leotta and Teddy laughed it off, fueling Digger's fire.

"O'Dell Burns! Burns Funeral!" Digger swung his feet back and forth, laughing hysterically. "Who in the hell would want to be buried at a place called Burns Funeral?"

O'Dell shook his head and kept walking past.

"No wonder Eternal Slumber has more business. Plus that little Emma Lee Raines sure has grown up to be a looker."

"That asshole," Jack Henry muttered, glancing back at Digger.

Digger pointed at him and laughed, getting Jack Henry's goat even more.

"Ignore him. It's his job to piss people off." I flung my arms around Jack Henry's neck and gave him a good long kiss.

"He's still a little jerk," Granny spat.

We continued to ignore Digger and he finally stopped making jokes about people he knew.

A few more minutes and Granny was back to her old self. A little bruised ego never hurt anyone. At least that was what we all told her. She was going to have to fight harder for mayor. With the election a week away, she was bound and determined to win.

After convincing everyone that I was all right, I kissed Jack Henry good night and walked back to Eternal Slumber.

It had been a long day and I needed some good sleep.

Little did I realize that wasn't going to happen tonight.

Middle-of-the-night door-knocking always scares the living bejesus out of me. It was hard to distinguish if it was a dream, Cephus's waking me up, or someone really at the door.

Bang, bang, bang!

Someone was really at the door.

Quickly, I jumped out of the bed and threw my sweatshirt over my head. The banging wasn't stopping, but it stopped my heart when I opened the door to find Jack Henry standing there in his police uniform.

"Oh my God!" I screamed. "Is it Granny? Is she okay? Charlotte Rae?"

When plain-clothed Jack Henry showed up at my door in the middle of the night, it was a very welcome sight. When uniform-clad Jack Henry showed up at any door in the middle of the night, everyone knew it was bad news.

"Do you have a minute?" Cop Jack Henry pushed his way into the small hallway.

I flipped on the light.

"Tell me. Tell me now." There was no need to sugarcoat it. Rip if off fast like a Band-Aid was what I was rooting for. "Is Granny hurt?"

"No. Zula Fae is fine. But our buddy Digger Spears." Jack Henry sucked in a deep breath. He took off his hat and stuck it under his armpit. "He's not doing as well."

"What does that mean?" I shook my head.

Even though I dated a cop, I still didn't get all of the cop lingo.

"He's dead." And just like that, he ripped off the Band-Aid. "He was found dead by another carnie."

"Really?" I leaned up against the wall. The sound of a death made me a little dizzy. "How?"

"He was floating in his tank of water." Jack rubbed his head.

"I guess Digger Spears should've learned to swim or hold his breath before he took that job." I tried to make a joke to get Jack Henry to smile. "Hey, I'm sorry. Do you want me to make some coffee?"

I turned to walk down the hall toward the kitchen.

"I'm not here on a social visit or in the need of some coddling." Jack Henry's voice was cold. "Digger didn't drown. He was stabbed."

"Damn." I turned back around. "What is going on with the world? Did some carnie get mad because Digger had a good gig and off him?"

"Someone got mad. I'm not so sure it was another carnie because it was a wooden stake." Jack Henry's face was stern. Serious. Scary.

"What was he? A vampire?" I joked, half-serious.

"It was a wooden stake attached to a VOTE FOR ZULA FAE RAINES PAYNE sign." Jack Henry's words and his body's coming toward me played out in slow motion as I fell to the ground.

Chapter 17

I wasn't sure how long I was out. All I knew was that Digger Spears was dead with one of Granny's campaign signs stuck right through his heart and it made Granny a suspect. Especially since she had fought with him.

"He made fun of the others too," I pointed out to Jack Henry, who stayed by my side.

He handed me a glass of ice water. "Please drink." Concern worked down his face and set at his jaw.

"I mean, O'Dell's business, and Teddy's muscle stuff." I took a drink.

"Neither O'Dell nor Teddy kept egging him on like Zula Fae did." Jack Henry just had to point that out.

I took another big sip. A door slammed in the front of the funeral home, followed by the clomping of heels.

"Shit." I put the glass down and looked at the clock. It was only seven in the morning and she's never here this early. "Charlotte Rae is here. She must know something."

The words had barely left my mouth when I heard Charlotte Rae raising all kinds of hell.

"Emma Lee!" she screamed, and banged on the door between my apartment and the hallway of the funeral home. "I know you and Jack Henry are in there. Open this damn door right now or I'm going to march right over to Sleepy Hollow Inn and drive a sign through Granny's heart!"

"She's mad." Jack Henry eased off the bed and walked out to let her in.

I breathed shallow so I could hear her when Jack Henry opened the door, but my heartbeat was almost too loud.

"Don't be sugarcoating anything for me, Jack Henry," Charlotte warned him. "You tell me how bad is it? I know it's real bad after the morning I have had."

"Calm down." Jack Henry had a voice of reason.

"Calm down my redheaded ass. Don't you tell me to calm down."

Enough was enough. I got out of bed and met them in the hallway.

"Damn, Emma Lee. Why can't you keep her on a leash? We are in dire straits now." Charlotte's face was as red as her hair. "You!" She jabbed her perfectly pink fingernail in Jack Henry's chest. "You stick her ass in jail and don't let her out!"

"I can't believe you have already put Digger Spears's murder on Granny." It took everything I had not to give her a good swift kick.

"Emma Lee is right. There were no prints on the sign. The homicide team is still working on collecting evidence." Jack Henry tried to calm her down.

"It doesn't do well for business. We already had a family cancel the viewing for next week and two pre-needs clients because they don't want to do business with murderers. One person claimed we killed people to get business." Charlotte stomped her foot.

"Excuse me." A quiet voice from behind startled us.

"My baby." Cephus grinned, taking in Mary Anna's look of the day. "She sure is a beaut."

Mary Anna had on a flirty dress that was knee length, belted at the waist, and tight on the top. She had on her signature heels. Today, her hair was pulled up in a pin, sweeping bangs, and a scarf to finish off the Marilyn look.

"I hate to break up this little family meeting, but I need to go downstairs to get my makeup." She pointed to the hallway leading to the funeral home.

"Jesus!" Charlotte threw her hands in the air. "Are you quitting?"

"No," she replied. "My services have been requested to do Digger Spears's makeup for the funeral."

"What? Are they using Burns?" Charlotte's anxiety level was turned way up too high.

Mary Anna didn't say anything. Her silence was all we needed.

"Oh my God! The least we could do is give them a free funeral." Charlotte glanced at me. One brow cocked. "You take care of that!" She jabbed her finger at me this time before she twirled on the tips of her high-heeled toes and stomped her way back down the hall.

"I don't think they are going to let you bury Digger with the sign and all." Mary Anna did an impression of someone's being stabbed with a stake in their heart and flung her tongue out the side of her mouth. "Besides, it's going to be a freak show anyway. They want me to paint his clown face on."

"Really?" Jack Henry seemed surprised.

I wasn't. There were always strange requests from families. The strangest I had had was where the family had hired a photographer and as a party prize to the mourners, they got a five-by-seven photo of them next to the deceased. Strange.

The noise of keys in the background was Charlotte Rae's unlocking all the doors.

"You know," she said. "That clown heckled so many people. There were Zula Fae signs all over. Anyone could've picked one up and stabbed the life right on out of him."

"He didn't deserve it." I shrugged. "Plus the fire at the mill and all."

"What does Digger Spears have to do with the fire?" Mary Anna's eyes narrowed. I could see the wheels turning and the gossip at the tip of her lips.

"Nothing." Jack Henry gave me the shut-the-hell-up look. "All this trauma in a few days isn't so good for Emma Lee."

"Right." Mary Anna's eyes grew big and she nodded. "I've gotta go."

"See ya." I smacked Jack Henry on the arm.

"Thanks. Now she's going to tell everyone that I've got a case of the Funeral Trauma."

"Good." Jack Henry seemed pleased with himself.

"Why is that good?"

"Now you can talk to Cephus out in public and get more clues from him. I'm about one-hundred-percent positive someone knows you are hot on the trail and they are trying to frame you."

Chapter 18

This is getting personal," I said to Cephus, who was sitting on the gurney in the back of the hearse. "Someone knows that I'm looking into your death. But who?"

"When times get tough, I say grab an ice-cold Stroh's." Cephus smacked his lips. He clicked the toes of his white, patent-leather shoes together.

"That would do nothing but make my mind all boggled. I have to figure out what happened to you."

"That's why I came." Cephus crossed his arms. "I didn't come down here to hang out with you for the rest of my ever after."

"It's not about you anymore. It's no longer

about getting you to the other side." I didn't mean to sound cold, there was too much at stake now. "It's about Granny. It's about the future of Eternal Slumber."

"Good. Maybe it's the motivation you need to solve my murder." Cephus looked out the window. "Hey! The Watering Hole is right up yonder!"

The cowboy boot looked even worse in the daylight. The rusted sign had visible wear and tear from years of being up. It was a staple. There was no way they could replace it though they could clean it up a bit.

"You are a doll baby." Cephus was practically drooling.

"Simmer down." I kept my eyes ahead of me. "Don't go and get all excited. We are on our way to Lexington." I pulled the pieces of paper out from underneath the seat. The ones I had taken from the old mill before someone wanted me to be the next victim.

The more I thought about it, the more it just didn't make sense. There weren't too many people who knew I had been asking around about Cephus. His family, Terk, the bartender, and maybe Vernon Baxter.

"I know you said that you didn't step out on Leotta." Stepping out was a nice way of saying "you low-down cheater, you." "But did you do any socializing that could have been seen as that?"

"I told you," he spat between his gritted teeth, "I never, not once, did I lay down with another woman."

"Then I think we are going to be safe to say that you were murdered over a gambling deal." It was definitely the only thing I could think of.

Like that, he disappeared into thin air.

"Good," I muttered. "I don't need you messing up my investigation with this newspaper guy."

I grabbed the gambling file from the seat and took out the piece of paper with letterhead of someone by the name of Fluggie Callahan. There was a newspaper clipping from the Lexington paper. The article was written by one Fluggie Callahan.

So I set the hearse on course to the *Lexington Herald Leader* in hopes Fluggie was still a reporter.

The Internet had definitely taken a toll on the print-newspaper business and most of the cubicles in the newspaper building were vacant—well, all but two.

"What can I do for you?" The woman in the closest cubicle pulled her glasses off her face and tucked the end of the frames in her mouth. She had sandy-blond hair that was pulled back in a scrunchie with several bobby pins keeping the sides in place. Her pale blue eyes matched her white-blond lashes. She dressed in a ridiculous pair of knee-length shorts with an elastic waist-band and a black T-shirt tucked in.

I held the file and article in my hand.

"I'm looking for a Fluggie Callahan." I held the article up.

"What do you want with Fluggie?" the lady asked.

She leaned on the edge of the cubicle wall, crossing a leg in front of her and resting it on the toe of her shoe.

"I wanted to ask him a few questions about his time as the only newspaper person, er, reporter"—I wasn't sure what they were called—"writer in Sleepy Hollow."

"First off"—she put her glasses back on her face and pushed them up to the bridge of her nose—"Fluggie is a woman. Secondly, you are looking at her."

"Oh. I'm so sorry." A nervous laughter left my body. "I'm obviously not an investigative reporter and I wasn't sure what gender Fluggie was."

In my gut, I felt like Fluggie and I were getting off on the wrong foot.

"I'm Emma Lee Raines." I stuck my hand out.

"Any kin to Eternal Slumber?" She eyed me with curiosity.

"Yes. How did you know?" I asked.

"Investigative reporter." She had a shit-eating grin on her face. "Say, isn't Zula Fae running for mayor down there?"

"Yes, but I'm here to ask about the gambling ring that you were looking into before the paper was shut down."

"Shut down?" She snickered. "The office was conveniently not for lease anymore and no one in town wanted to even talk to me when I came in to ask for space. I was pushed out."

"Do you know by who? Or why?" I asked.

"Why all the sudden interest, Ms. Raines?" She eased down into her computer chair. It squeaked as she got comfortable. She drummed her fingers together in front of her face.

"I need to talk with some of the bookies and I was trying to pick up where you left off." I handed her the file, which really didn't have any leads in it. "I found that in the old mill right before someone didn't want me to find it and blew the place to smithereens."

"I heard about that." She was cool as a cucumber. Her eyes assessing me. "What is in this for me?"

"For starters, my gratitude." I used Granny's saying it was easier to catch flies with honey than vinegar water.

"Honey"—she pulled back her fingers from her face and neatly placed them in her lap—"gratitude doesn't pay the bills. What do you have that is better than feelings?"

"I don't have anything." I bit my lip. No wonder Fluggie was driven out of town. Being nasty gets you nowhere.

"You do. You just aren't using your noggin'." She pointed to her head. "Your Granny has a platform she's running on right?"

"Yes."

"I want my newspaper back. My little Sleepy Hollow paper." She was driving a hard bargain.

"What if Granny doesn't win?" I asked.

"Then you have to do your damnedest to get O'Dell Burns to open it back up." She pushed her chair back and it hit the cubicle wall.

"And what if I can't do that?" I asked.

"We'll settle up somehow. But I've got faith in you, Emma Lee Raines. You look like a go-getter. You are on a mission." She bit her lip. She watched my facial expression like cop Jack Henry did. "Obviously, someone didn't want you to find my old files that I clearly cared nothing for or I would have taken them with me. They don't like your meddling. So . . ." she paused, " . . . what gives?"

Ahem. I cleared my throat. I knew I wasn't going

to be able to tell her I was a Betweener so I chose my words carefully.

"My friend and employee, Mary Anna Hardy, has been investigating the disappearance of her father—"

She interrupted, "Cephus Hardy. Town drunk."

"You know Cephus?" I was a bit in shock.

"Yeah." Her mouth opened slightly. Her tongue coiled back, playing with her molars. Her nose curled. "I was getting close to uncovering that gambling ring and I think he's a key player. I got a few warnings. He disappeared. I got evicted."

"He's still not back and his family is wanting answers."

"And they hired you. An undertaker?" The creases between her eyes deepened.

"Yes." I kept a steady face. "So are you going to give me your leads?"

"And get you killed?" She harrumphed. "No chance in hell. But." She stood up. "I'll be willing to assist you so I can make sure you keep up your end of the deal."

"Listen, I told you," I backed up, "I can't guarantee the paper will reopen."

"If you and I solve this gambling ring and find Cephus Hardy, they will have to reopen it." She pushed back toward a fax-machine-type box and took off the paper that had printed. She read the paper and held it up. "Does your little visit have anything to do with the death of a clown from a carnival in Sleepy Hollow that just so happened to have been killed by a stake through his heart that was attached to a ZULA FOR MAYOR sign?"

"It might have upped the ante, but it wasn't the original drive." I figured I better not tell Fluggie a lie. She seemed to be good at her job. "Do you think the shutdown of the paper had anything to do with the gambling ring?"

"Do we have a deal?" She wasn't going to answer any questions until I had agreed to get the paper back in Sleepy Hollow.

"I'll try my hardest." I was serious. I would go to the town council with a proposal to restart the paper if I had to, but it wasn't going to be easy.

There was a long silence. I had learned from Jack Henry that during investigations, you sometimes had to be quiet. Let the silence play out. See if the other folds. Unfortunately, I didn't have all day and Fluggie seemed to be the one with all the time in the world. She eased back in the chair and crossed her arms across her chest. She pulled her leg up and rested her ankle on her other knee.

"Yes." I gave in. "I'll get them to start the paper up."

I didn't know how I was going to do it but I was

going to if it meant getting Granny off the hook and saving the funeral home. The thought of how Charlotte Rae would hold it over my head was even more motivation.

"Yes. There isn't any proof about the shutdown of the paper being correlated with the gambling ring." She pulled out a long cabinet drawer and used her fingers to dance over the tabs until she reached the file she was looking for. She pulled out a piece of paper with her handwriting on it. "One of the last things I uncovered was the names of the local bookies before Cephus Hardy kicked me out."

"Cephus Hardy kicked you out of where?" I asked.

"The old mill. He and his old lady own it." Fluggie shook her head and put the piece of paper back in the file. She gave the drawer a little shove and it slowly clicked shut. "You didn't even know that the old mill belonged to the man you are trying to find?"

A little embarrassed, I shook my head.

"You see what you can find out about the paper and I'll look into these bookies." She grabbed the mug off her desk and a business card off her keyboard. "I'm going to get some stale coffee."

She handed me the card.

"Call me when you find something out." She walked past me and down the hall.

She didn't ask for my number or how to get in touch with me. I wasn't going to let a little oversight on figuring out who owned the old mill bring me down. I looked down the hallway, both ways, and I was alone. It was a good time to look at that file.

I barely squeezed the handle open, so not to click, and pulled the file drawer out. I started thumbing through the files until I reached the one labeled "Sleepy Hollow Gamble." I kept the file sticking halfway out of the drawer so I wouldn't lose the spot. I grabbed the piece of paper she had pulled out.

She had three names and numbers scribbled on it. It had to be the three bookies she was talking about. I grabbed a pen and ripped a piece of sticky notes from her desk and wrote the names and numbers down before placing the piece of paper back in the drawer and slowly shutting it.

There was a conversation in the back of the building, which I could only assume was Fluggie and another reporter. There wasn't much time to get out of there. I slipped around the cubicle wall and headed out the door.

Chapter 19

There were two things I had learned from my little visit with Fluggie Callahan. Well, three.

The most important to the investigation were the names and numbers of the bookies. The second most important was that Leotta Hardy owned the old-mill property. And third, Cephus Hardy had good timing when he chose to disappear.

On the way back to Eternal Slumber, I thought about why Leotta would want me to keep silent. Did she kill her own husband?

I mean, it really wasn't that far-fetched. Over and over you hear that the spouse was the first suspect and generally was the one with the motive to kill.

And it seemed Leotta did have a motive. One,

Cephus was a drunk. Two, Cephus was obviously a gambler. And if Vernon Baxter and Leotta were in fact having an affair, it would be a way to get Cephus out of the picture.

My phone chirped a text from my back pocket. At the stoplight right before I turned to circle the square, I pulled it out to see who it was.

"Ugh." A bad taste filled my mouth when I saw it was Charlotte and she wanted to know if I had gotten to talk to the Spears family about the free funeral.

Instead of turning toward the funeral home, I went straight through the light, passing the cemetery, and taking a left into the trailer park.

There was nothing funnier than a hearse's pulling down the main road of a trailer park. The sounds of front screen doors slammed as I passed and the owners hung over their small porch railings to see exactly where the hearse was going to stop. Even a few kiddos hopped on their bikes and followed the dust the wheels of the hearse had created.

I rolled down the windows and rested my elbow on the sill, giving a few waves as I passed the wondering eyes. In the rearview mirror, I could see the neighbors gathered in the middle of the street, pointing and gossiping. Probably taking bets on who had died.

I eased around the corner to the back of the park, where the Spears's double-wide sat on a two-lot spot. It was a lot of money to rent two lots. They had to pay double the water, double the electric, double the rent and I was sure a free funeral could help out.

Their trailer was in the dead center of the lots. There was a small lattice fence that went around the base of the white-and-orange-striped trailer. They had a bigger front porch, with a steel awning running across the top. An old, beat-up couch sat on the front porch along with a small table. Mrs. Spears stood up. The old nylon 1980s jogging suit was a bit faded as well as her white, cracked, K-Swiss tennis shoes. Her dishwater-colored hair was in a messy knot at the base of her neck and dark circles had found a home under each of her eyes. She took a long draw on her cigarette and let out a steady stream of smoke before she realized I was stopping at her house.

She went to the door and yelled something. Moments later, Mr. Spears came to the door. He had on a pair of cutoff blue-jeans shorts showing off his stick legs, his big naked belly flopped over the front, hiding the button and zippers that I was sure were strained and taut.

I grabbed some Eternal Slumber literature out

of the glove box and got out. Mr. Spears gestured for Mrs. Spears to give him her cigarette. She did and he took a draw off it before he flicked it in the yard toward me.

"What do you want?" Mr. Spears growled. That was not happiness to see me. "Don't you think your family has done enough to us?"

"I'm sorry about what happened to Digger." I thought a little empathy went a long way. Boy was I wrong.

"Git ya skinny little ass out of here!" He flung his finger to the front of the park. "Before I go and git my gun!"

I put my hands out in front of me.

"I really am sorry. I just wanted to know if we can offer you a free service and burial for Digger." I threw in the free plot at the cemetery. Charlotte Rae was going to die about that, but it's better than her having to stick me in the ground.

"We don't need your charity." He spat. "Our boy hadn't been back since he graduated high school. He was going to come here for dinner last night but looks like your Granny ruined it. Look at my wife. She's heartbroken."

Mrs. Spears never said a word. She lit another cigarette and eased back on the old couch.

"O'Dell Burns is going to give our boy the send-off he needs for free." His words stung. "I hope that Granny of yours rots in hell for what she did to my boy!"

"I told you to stay in the shadow!" Cephus warned someone next to the trailer.

I gulped. I choked. I almost died right then and there when I saw the ghost of Digger Spears standing next to the ghost of Cephus Hardy.

"Umm . . ." I turned around. I had to get out of there. "Have a good day."

"And you can tell Zula Fae that we have changed our vote to O'Dell Burns for mayor!" Mrs. Spears screamed at me.

I jumped in the hearse and pulled the gear down as quickly as I could.

"Shit! Shit!" I gulped and sped through the trailer park. "This is not happening," I prayed, and repeated, "this is not happening."

"It's not happening. It happened." The voice of Digger Spears was eerily too close.

"You are not here." I squeezed my eyes shut before I looked over.

Digger Spears sat next to me in the passenger seat. Clown makeup and all.

Cephus sat cross-legged on the church truck.

"I tried to tell him not to show himself because you were a little sensitive to helping us, but he insisted that y'all were friends and you'd help solve his murder first." Cephus rolled his eyes.

"So, have you always had this talent?" Digger was interested in my other job.

"No." I gripped the wheel and took a left out of the trailer park. I had to get to Jack Henry. Not only to tell him about Digger's ghost, but I had to talk to someone who genuinely cared about me and knew that I wasn't going nuts. "I don't want to talk about it."

"Just one question." He held his finger up in the air. My silence must've been his go-ahead. "You really didn't have the Funeral Trauma like my momma said?"

"No." My hands hurt from how tight they held on to the wheel. The pain made me feel real, alive. A little less crazy. "Your mother told you about that?"

"Hell ya. We thought you lost your marbles." He did a shimmy shake. "The thought of your seeing ghosts is creepy."

"Your having a job as a traveling clown is creepy." My body relaxed a little. I guess I felt like I was just talking to Digger, not the ghost. "Besides, I'm helping you get to the other side."

"I told you that she's called a Betweener." Cephus's nerves were running thin. "He's dumber than a box of rocks. No wonder he could only get a job as a clown."

"Listen here, you drunk . . ." Digger started, but I interrupted.

"You listen." I let go of the wheel with one hand and pointed between them. "I won't have ghost-fighting going on here. If you want my help, you have to follow my rules."

I had never had to put in ground rules, but there was a first for everything.

"First rule, I ask the questions, you answer. No back talk and absolutely no fighting between you two." I sighed deeply. "There might be more rules to come."

Both of them eyed each other before they both did some sort of wrestling move.

"I'm not kidding," I warned. "Or you both will be in the between forever because I'm good at ignoring now."

They seemed to listen to that last warning. They knew I was their only hope.

Chapter 20

Is Jack Henry here?" I asked the dispatch officer when I walked into the Sleepy Hollow police station—Cephus and Digger in tow. "I really need to see him."

The dispatch officer must've heard the urgency in my voice because she never told me where he was if he was out and about. She looked around and when the coast was clear, she leaned out the small, sliding-glass window.

She whispered, "Honey, he went to see your Granny. I don't think it's looking good."

"Thanks." I tapped the ledge of the window and skipped right out the door.

"What did that mean?" Digger asked.

"It means Zula Fae is being charged with your murder." Digger was catching on quickly to how this Betweener gig worked.

"Zula Fae didn't kill me." He shook his head. "She couldn't have hit me that hard."

"What do you mean hit you?" My eyes slid his way. "You were stabbed in the heart."

"That was after they hit me from behind."

"Wait. What? Start over," I coaxed him.

"The night was over. A buddy who has the strong-arm booth." He flexed. "I really wanted the strong-arm booth, but I had to work my way up in the ranks. First, I worked at the fill the balloon with water game."

"Stay on task," I encouraged him.

"Oh, yeah." He looked out the window. "Anyway, Gus, the strong-armed man, brought me over a beer. For good luck, all the workers end their night by sitting at their booths and drinking a beer." He shrugged. "I always get off the dunking board, but I wanted to look around Sleepy Hollow since it was my town. So I was enjoying my beer, feet dangling, and pretty proud to have seen all y'all. It was fun." He smacked his hands together, causing me to jump. "Then whack! My head felt like it had exploded. I fell forward. I think I drowned from being knocked out."

"They haven't finished the autopsy." I wondered where they stood with that.

"I just floated right on out of my body." Digger lifted his arms in the air. "Do you remember standing in a doorway when we were kids and putting our hands on each side, pressing as hard as we could, and when we stepped away, our arms floated up in the air?"

"Yes." I smiled, fond memories.

"That's how it felt, but my whole body." He grinned. There was peace in his eyes.

"So, who killed you? Because I'm sure whoever killed you killed Cephus." That was how this thing was playing out. "And now they are after me."

"That's the strange thing." He looked over at me, his eyes hollow, haunted. "I focused on my body and didn't see who was busy stabbing the sign through my heart."

Before I asked any more questions in fear I'd look crazy to all the people walking around the square, I turned on the radio, pretending to sing when I pulled back around the square.

"Did you see anything?" I sang.

"No." He hung his head. "I'm sorry, Emma Lee. I sure wish we had the opportunity to grab that beer."

"An ice-cold Stroh's would be good right about

now. It'd help my nerves since this clown is dancing on them." Cephus snarled at Digger.

I pulled next to Jack Henry's cop car in the parking of the Sleepy Hollow Inn.

He must've been watching out the window of the Inn because he beat me to the car before I even got out.

"Emma Lee, now is not a good time." Jack Henry held the corner of the hearse door.

"Now is as good as a time as ever," I whispered. "Since I now have Cephus Hardy *and* Digger Spears to deal with. What did Digger's autopsy turn up?"

"Parents didn't want an autopsy," Jack Henry stated.

"He needs an autopsy." My mouth dropped. "I thought all murders got an autopsy."

"He was obviously stabbed to death. It doesn't take an autopsy to figure that out. Saves money."

"Damn, Jack Henry. Do your job!" I grunted. "Spend the money. Tell the parents. Mark my words, Digger Spears was knocked out from behind with something. He fell into the water pit and drowned. Someone stabbed him to set up Granny."

"Is that what he said?"

"He knows about the Between shit?" Digger

stood next to Jack Henry and waved his hand in front of Jack Henry's face. "Can he see me?"

"No." I shook my head.

"No, he didn't?" Jack Henry sighed.

"Yes to you." I pointed to Jack Henry. "Yes, Digger, he knows about the Betweener stuff and no he can't see you."

"You trusted a cop? A pig? A narc? A rat?" Digger snarled, flexing his arms.

"Numbnuts, they are an item." Cephus did kissy sounds in the air.

"Focus on me, Emma Lee." Jack Henry's patience was running thin. "His parents are demanding an arrest. An arrest of Zula Fae."

"You can't do that." I was becoming increasingly angry. "I understand what it looks like, but you have to trust me."

"Listen, I'm going to bring in Zula for questioning, just to have it on the record." He bent down and, in his low Southern drawl, said, "You get these two to give you some real clues into their murders. Don't go investigate, just get the clues, give them to me. That is how you are going to help Zula Fae." He stood back up. "In the meantime, I'll send someone over to talk to the Spearses to get them to take another look at an autopsy. Understand?"

"Can't you just have Vernon Baxter take a look at him since we know he didn't kill Cephus?" I asked, testing his limits.

"Understand, Emma Lee?" He wasn't budging.

My lips pursed to keep me from arguing. I nodded, giving him the answer he wanted but not what my actions were going to be.

He shut the door and walked back up the steps of the Inn. I quickly called Hettie Bell and asked her to please take over the Inn while Granny was at the police station getting questioned. She didn't hesitate.

"Now where are we going?" Digger and Cephus asked in unison.

"Eternal Slumber." I sighed. "I have to tell Charlotte Rae about your funeral plans."

"What about my funeral plans?" Cephus asked.

"Your family doesn't know you are dead. They think you're still alive, gone on your own. That's why we have to find something of your body besides the ring." Those words were going to sting him. "Do you think Leotta could've . . . killed you?"

"Are you crazy?" Cephus spat and disappeared.

"What's his problem?" Digger asked.

"He's a touchy ghost. He likes to disappear at the wrong time." I stared out the windshield and pulled into the funeral-home lot.

With Digger next to me, I knew he wasn't going anywhere. He was going to stick to me like glue.

"Hey there." I pushed open Charlotte Rae's office door. "Burns gave the Spears a free funeral too."

"You didn't work hard enough." Charlotte's beautiful white teeth gnashed.

"I did. I even threw in a free burial." I knew that would get her attention.

"Holy hell, they're really holding Granny against us." She pounded the desk.

"You better stop before you break a nail," I joked, hoping to get on with my investigation.

"We have to separate Granny's image from the funeral home." Charlotte pushed her chair back and walked her lanky body over to the window. "How? You come up with cleaver ideas. How are we going to do that?" She turned and looked at me.

"Hire some sort of firm that cleans up these sort of messes." I didn't have time but I wasn't about to tell her that.

"Great idea." She rushed back to her seat. "Shut the door. I need to make a few calls."

That was all I needed to hear to get the hell out of there and find Leotta. It was a stop I didn't want to make, but I needed some real answers about her relationship with Cephus. Seeing her was the only way.

"Hi, Emma Lee." The voice startled me. Vernon Baxter was standing by the elevator.

"Vernon. Oh God, Vernon, I'm so sorry about the whole Cephus ring and all," I apologized. "It's just that when I was checking out your garden, I saw his ring and knew I had recognized it. Mary Anna told me her dad never took it off. And his disappearance and all . . ."

"No big deal, Emma Lee. I get it." He was gaunt; his face tired. He slouched a little. "I'm just glad I was cleared."

"Great." Hmm . . . I wondered how Jack Henry cleared him. "What are you doing here?"

"I'm checking the machine. I heard there was a young boy from here that traveled with the circus that was stabbed to death." As a good Southern gentleman, Vernon left off the main detail of the weapon's being Granny's sign.

"Is that all you heard?" I asked in a joking tone.

"Emma Lee, you know I don't pack tales." He smiled back. "Besides, you know and I know that Zula Fae might talk a big talk, but when it comes down to it, she'd never hurt a fly, let alone a human."

"Do you have a minute to talk?" It was time I came clean with Vernon.

"Sure." He got in the elevator and I followed.

"I really didn't come to your house so I could make sure you had some ZULA FAE FOR MAYOR stuff."

"I figured that."

"Oh, I guess I'm not good at lying." A half smile formed on my lips.

"I'm listening." He stepped off the elevator and held the door with one hand so it wouldn't shut on me.

"Anyway, I've been thinking about Teddy and Mary Anna's daddy since Teddy was in town and it just seemed weird for Cephus to disappear like that." I pretended to straighten up the inventory stocked down there so I didn't have to look at him.

"And I guess you heard from all the gossip queens around here about my run-in with Cephus the day he disappeared?"

"Yeah, something like that." I wasn't about to tell him that Cephus told me. For obvious reasons.

"Leotta deserves better than him. She put up with him stumbling in late at night. Spending every dime they had on gambling." Vernon's voice was strong and steady. "He needed to do right by his kids and I told him that."

"Tell me about the gambling."

"All Leotta told me was how Cephus would work odd jobs here and there, plus work a little for

Terk Rhinehammer on the side, making decent money as a stonemason down at the water plant."

"I had no idea Cephus was a bricklayer." I wondered why Cephus didn't hold down a steady job.

"He sure was. Best one in town. But people didn't want to hire him because after they'd pay him, he wouldn't show up to finish the job or he would show up too drunk to finish the job." He didn't hide his disapproval of Cephus. "Leotta or Teddy would finish the job. It would make me so mad. Leotta never once wanted to leave him. As much as I begged her to bring the kids to live with me, she wouldn't listen. Though they were hardly kids at the time. Mary Anna was on her own and Teddy was a senior."

"I'm not sure what your relationship with Leotta is now, but do you think she might have killed Cephus?" I asked.

"Hell no." He scratched his head. "I never thought about it though. I guess we just always believed he got drunk and left. Do you think he's dead?"

"Nah." I waved off his question, realizing I had already said too much. "I just think someone knows I'm asking questions and that someone wants me dead or hurt and they know Granny is the way to my heart."

"I heard about the old mill." He looked down

at the ringing phone's caller ID. "Sleepy Hollow police," he said before he picked up the phone to say hello.

I digested what he had told me about Cephus. I had no clue, nor was Cephus going to confess to the gambling and all the drinking.

"That was Jack Henry." He had a surprised look on his face. "He just asked me to do an autopsy on Digger Spears per the law. Seems there's more to his death than a stake through his heart."

"Is that right?" I asked with a straight face, but my soul was smiling. I was glad to think Jack Henry informed Digger's parents of the law, though I was sure it was hard for him. I made a mental note to give Jack Henry the best kiss of his life when I saw him.

I took out my phone and quickly texted him. *Dinner tonight. My place. Make up for last time. No protective covering. And I don't just mean the ice layering.* I added a winky face emoticon.

Quickly he answered. *Sounds like a date! I'm willing to skip dinner . . . Be there by 7.*

Seven? I glanced down at the time on the phone. I only had a few hours and a lot of questions to be answered by a lot of people.

"Let me know what you find out." I said goodbye and shot back up in the elevator.

I could hear Charlotte Rae telling somebody about the big mess Granny had gotten us into. With the autopsy, I knew Granny was going to be exonerated of involvement in Digger's murder. But I left Charlotte Rae alone. It would keep her out of my hair.

Since we didn't have any clients or anyone banging on the door for pre-need arrangements, I was going to spend my time wisely.

"Who first?" I looked out over the square, weighing my options.

I had a list of bookies, Leotta, another visit with Mary Anna—who I thought would be the best option to ask about the old mill, and I was going to try Terk Rhinehammer again to see if he had any leads.

The carnival was still going strong. They put a black sheet around the dunk both with R.I.P spray-painted in big red letters.

"Anyone want to arm wrestle?" The loud voice echoed through the carnival and over to the steps of Eternal Slumber.

"Yes, Gus. I think I do." I confirmed before I trotted down the steps and made my way over to the carnival.

Chapter 21

"Step right up, little lady." Gus flexed. Veins and muscles popped out of places on his arm where they shouldn't.

Inwardly, I groaned. He wasn't the type of man I liked, but many women swooned, especially the few that had gathered around his booth.

"Tell Gus who you want me to arm wrestle." He made sure he was loud and clear over the speaker.

"Me," I whispered.

He moved the microphone away from his mouth. "I think I heard you say me."

"Yes. Me," I confirmed.

"Well, little lady." His voice was booming over the speakers. "I'm a gentleman. Plus these country boys around here wouldn't like me taking advantage of a nice sweet young lady such as yourself."

"Tell me about Digger Spears and I'll leave you alone."

I looked at his watch.

"Ladies and gentlemen, even the strongman has to take a break every once in a while." He stuck a Velcro sign on the pole of his booth that read BE BACK SOON.

"Listen here, I don't know what kind of stunt you want to pull but you need to be on your way." Gus's nice demeanor had quickly vanished. "We are doing our best to carry on with business as usual."

"All I wanted to know was if Digger had any issues with anyone in the group? You know, someone who might have wanted to kill him?" It seemed like a reasonable question.

Maybe I was wrong. Maybe Digger's murder wasn't related to Cephus.

"No one. Everyone loved the kid." Gus's gentler side was coming back. "We did a lot of friendly banter back and forth about wrestling and all."

"I was a little surprised to see him be a clown." I glanced over at Digger, who was standing next to his booth. I wished he had come over to help with the line of questioning, but he didn't see Gus or any other carnie as a threat.

"Yeah, he said something about—" Gus stopped when someone interrupted.

"I'm not paying you to find a piece of ass." The man growled. He was obviously the guy in charge. "Now get back to work. And you." He pointed to me. "I saw you shaking your thing around my dunk tank last night. Get on out of here!"

"I'm—"

"I'm nothing. Get out of here before I call the police and have you arrested for loitering." He stomped back to the little trailer, which I assumed held the carnival office space.

Gus didn't look twice. He put the headset back on and took down the sign and was already arm wrestling his next victim.

"You should never mess with Big Mike. He takes the carnival business pretty serious." Digger decided to join me across the street as I walked down to Artie's Meat and Deli to grab some food to make for my romantic dinner with Jack Henry.

I cleared my throat to let Digger know that I heard him but couldn't respond. The Auxiliary women were standing in front of Artie's with VOTE FOR ZULA signs.

"Thank you so much for doing this for Granny." I had to put differences aside with Beulah Paige for the sake of Granny. These women were her friends and she needed them right now.

"Honey." Mable Claire rattled up to me. She stuck her hand in her pocket and took out the most awful sight of coins I ever did see. "I know it's not much, but use this on Zula's bond money."

"Bond money?" I laughed and pushed her hand away. "Granny doesn't need bond money."

"She don't?" Sarcasm dripped out of Beulah Paige's perfectly lined lips.

I looked over the square to see what everyone was looking at.

Granny was on her moped, whizzing through the carnival crowd with her white flag flying high behind her. She was going full throttle. The little red hair sticking out of her aviator helmet blew in the wind and the goggles magnified her eyes.

Wheeee, wheeeee, the scooter whined.

"Zula Fae, you get back here right now!" Jack Henry was doing his best to keep up with her. He shook his fist in the air. "I'm going to arrest you for not cooperating with the law!" he screamed even louder.

"Good gravy." I hid my eyes when I saw Granny's moped fly by Eternal Slumber and Charlotte Rae standing on the front porch.

Charlotte Rae burst out into tears and ran back in the funeral home. I turned to face the Auxiliary women. They had leaned their signs up against the outside of Artie's.

"We just can't condone this sort of behavior." That was Beulah Paige's nice way of saying they didn't associate with crazy. "So we are just gonna go on in Higher Grounds for a glass of refreshing iced tea."

They passed by me one by one, without eye contact.

The cashier at Artie's had her face planted up against the store window, taking in all to see. She wasn't above gossip when store customers came in and this little episode would definitely qualify as the headline gossip for the day . . . maybe even the week . . . hell, the month.

My phone chimed in a text. It was Charlotte saying she has gone home to go to bed. Granny had done her in. And that Leotta Hardy had stopped by to see me. I texted her back with a smiley face. She sent back *fuck off and take care of YOUR granny.*

Granny deserved to stay a night in jail—that

was if Jack Henry caught up with her. She was a sneaky, little, old broad and could fit in the smallest of places.

Besides, Jack Henry would tell me all about it at dinner, which was just a short time away.

I grabbed up some steaks, potatoes, butter beans, corn-bread mix, and a bag of salad for tonight's dinner. The cashier didn't say two words to me. If she would've, Jack Henry might have gotten a call about me; and then I'd be sharing a cell with Granny.

Besides, my mind was elsewhere. I wondered what Leotta wanted. Was she on my trail? Did Vernon tell her that I asked if she was guilty of murder?

Chapter 22

Leotta Hardy lived past the old mill in the country. The last thing I wanted to do was drive all the way out there after I had almost been killed.

I recognized the Buick. It was the same one that had been in front of Higher Grounds, Terk's Buick. The redbrick ranch house had cracks running down the bricks. The black shutters were in need of a new paint job. They had faded to a dull gray and a couple of them were hanging by one nail. A couple of the window screens had slashes down them and a couple more lay in the yard. Maybe that was what Leotta was going for.

She could've gotten out and weeded the front bushes or even trimmed them up. They toppled into each other and above the windowsill. Long weeds grew up and around each bush.

Maybe right now wasn't a great time to see what she wanted, but it was now or never. There was no way I was going to drive back out here. She wanted to talk to me, now was the time.

I knocked on the door for a few minutes before I noticed the dingy curtain in the window on the front door part. I heard the sound of a bolt sliding open along with another click.

I guess when you lived this far out, it was better to be safe than sorry. By the looks of things, she never left the house or even walked out the door.

"Hi-do, Emma Lee." Leotta's lips set in a tight line. "You can come on in. I was expecting you."

She opened the door wide. I stepped in. Terk Rhinehammer was seated at the table that was right inside the door.

I was happy to see that the inside of the house was much nicer than the outside. Maybe nicer was pushing it. Let's say that I didn't see anything broken though she could've dusted or swept the floor.

A couple of cats darted about, knocking the lid to a twenty-ounce Coke bottle between them. They darted under the table and knocked off a picture frame.

I bent down to pick it up and put it back. I was expecting to see a picture of one of her children or even Cephus. Wrong. It was Marilynn Monroe's infamous picture of the dress flying up as she stood on top of the grate.

"Damn," Cephus ran his fingers through those thick curls of his. "She's let them nasty cats in. I never would've let that happen."

"Hello." I smiled and sat in the seat next to Terk.

Leotta cha-chaed over to the refrigerator. She pulled the door open, bent over and looked in.

She wasn't dressed as conservatively as she was at Higher Grounds. Today she was dressed more like Mary Anna. Tight short cutoffs and a V-neck wife beater. Her breasts tumbled over the top. No wonder where Mary Anna got her fashion sense.

Over her shoulder, she called, "Anyone want a beer?"

"Yep." Terk threw his finger in the air, then drew it down to me. "You?"

"No thank you." I shook my head.

There was no way I was going to drink anything that might impair my ability though one drink wouldn't. I had to be on alert at all times.

"Oh no," Cephus cried out when he saw Leotta take out a can of PBR. "She's lost her mind since I've died."

Ahem. I cleared my throat, giving him the signal to hush.

Cephus paced back and forth, his white, patent-leather shoes clicking with each step.

"Them sum-bitches," Leotta spat, and sat in the open seat across from me. "Vernon Baxter did not kill Cephus."

"Though he did have reason." Terk patted Leotta's hand.

I noticed she jerked away and took a swig of beer.

"I came to see you today to let you know that." Her beady black eyes zeroed in on mine. It was hard for me to not look away.

"Go on, tell her," Terk encouraged her. "I know that you took that piece of paper off my table when you came to campaign for Zula Fae." His eyes lowered.

He was onto me.

"Well, Mary Anna has been worried about her mom and she really wanted to know Cephus's whereabouts. That's all." I tapped my fingers on the table. "I was just trying to help her."

"That's why I hired Terk." Leotta pointed the bottle at Terk before she took another swig.

She got up and squeezed past Terk's chair and the wall, giving Terk some eyelash fluttering. I swear there was a little drool in the corner of his lip.

"I'll take another one, babe." Terk held up the empty bottle.

"Don't call me babe," she warned Terk, and pulled out two more beers before she sashayed back to her seat. "Terk has been hot on the trail of Cephus's bookie. But you seemed to have gotten that list. Plus Beulah Paige Bellefry asked me if Cephus was back because you told Doc Clyde he was."

I kept my mouth shut.

"I want you to know about me and Vern." She took a deep breath. Her lungs filled. Her boobs inflated and pulled the wife beater tick tight. "Vern is a good man. There was nothing between us then. In fact, I had set him up on several dates with Bea Allen. But that didn't work out. Lucky for me because now me and Vern are a different story." She held the bottle up to her lips as she talked. "A girl has needs and Cephus isn't here to give me my needs."

There was a whole lot of ewww in my head. My nose curled at the thought of what she was trying to tell me.

"Hmm." Terk's displeasure was apparent. He rolled his eyes. "Keep going, let Emma Lee decide."

"Decide what?" I asked.

"Cephus threatened Vernon the day he went over there. He was going to blackmail him," Terk blurted.

Leotta smacked him in the arm. He winced and put up a shoulder barrier to her.

Blackmail was a pretty good reason to kill someone. I didn't say it out loud but she wasn't helping Vernon's cause.

"I wasn't going to really blackmail him. Just a warning." Cephus huffed like a little baby.

"What do you mean by blackmail?" I asked, encouraging Leotta to tell me.

"Cephus had it in his mind that I was cheating on him with Vernon." Her eyes hooded. "I wasn't. I just want to make that clear."

"You have made it very clear." I nodded.

"Cephus had dug into Vernon's past because he said that someone as young as Vernon just doesn't move to a place like Sleepy Hollow because they retired." She tapped the table with the bottom of the beer bottle. "Cephus was pretty good at knowing the strangest things. He was right. Vernon had been brought up on charges at his last job as a county coroner in Tennessee."

"What?" I shook my head. Before Vernon Baxter

was hired at Eternal Slumber, there was a background check on him that turned up nothing.

"Yep." Terk's lips pushed out like a duck's. "Criminal."

"He's not a criminal. It was the people working for him. They were taking the organs out of the dead and selling them to labs all over the United States for research." Leotta let it all roll out of her mouth. "He didn't know a thing about it until the Feds showed up and arrested him."

"Are you sure?" I asked.

"Betcha one thousand dollars I'm sure." She stuck her hand out like I was going to take her up on that bet.

And who had the gambling problem?

She drew her hand back. "The Feds didn't find anything on Vernon and he cooperated with them by going undercover and getting his employees to let him in on the action. After a few months, they let him do a drop of a heart. That's when it all went down."

"He didn't get charged with anything?" I wanted to make it one-hundred-percent clear so I could tell Jack Henry.

"Not a thing. He didn't do nothin'; I told you." Leotta's words were starting to slur. Her body slumped back in the chair. "It gets my goat every time I think about Cephus trying to blackmail Vernon. Vernon told Cephus to tell the world that he wasn't charged. But if I know Cephus, he probably kept on and on."

"Did not." Cephus folded his arms in front of him and looked away. His words weren't so convincing.

"Vernon said that he and Cephus had words in the garden because he was gardening when Cephus stormed over there. The phone inside Vernon's house rang and he went inside to get it. When he came back out, Cephus was gone," Leotta said.

"Did he tell you who called him?" I asked.

"He said it was a hang up." She drank the last bit of beer in the bottle, which looked like backwash to me.

"Are you in love with Vernon Baxter?" I asked.

Leotta drew back. "Why Emma Lee Raines, I don't think that's any of your business."

"If Cephus was right and there was something between you and Vernon like you alluded to, then it gives you motive to get rid of Cephus." I stood up because I knew what I was about to say was going to get me kicked out on my ass. "Cephus spent all your money on his ice-cold Stroh's and if there was anything left over, he used it to gamble. Are you sure you want to find his bookie to see if he did anything to Cephus or do you want to see if Cephus had any money coming to him? Where is Cephus, Leotta?"

"I don't like what you are implying, Emma Lee." Leotta pounded her fist on the table. "I think it's time you let yourself out."

I did what she said.

"I told you she wasn't going to help you," I overheard Terk say when the door slammed behind me.

My mind hurt when I left Leotta's. She had said a lot in a little bit of time. It was true that the information Cephus had on Vernon wasn't anything to blackmail him over. But it did give motive for Leotta to do something and it was definitely something more for me to look into before Leotta got in touch with Mary Anna.

Mary Anna and her momma were tight. If I accused Leotta of something she didn't do, Mary Anna would be all piss and vinegar on me. That was a headache I didn't need. But it was information Jack Henry could use.

I was past the point of exhaustion by the time I pulled into Eternal Slumber, so I stuck the steaks on the small portable grill on the outside of the funeral home and grabbed a beer from the fridge. Tonight, Cephus and Digger's murderer was going to have to wait.

There was no room left in my head to fit any more nonsense and clues that didn't add up. I needed a night off and that was going to be spent with Jack Henry.

"Aren't you going to ask me about your granny?" We almost made it through dinner without either of us talking about it.

"Nope." I picked up the empty beer bottle, threw it in the trash and grabbed another out of my minifridge.

I unscrewed the top and took a nice long swig.

"Too bad that's not an ice-cold Stroh's." Cephus smacked his lips next to me.

"Nice of you to show up in this little investigation of ours." I had reached my tolerance limit with my Betweener clients or I had reached my alcohol-consumption limit. Either way, I was done with them for the night. "I'm sick and tired of your disappearing whenever you feel like it. I need answers. I need them now and if you don't produce some soon, then I'm all done helping your ass!" I screamed at the top of my lungs.

"Emma Lee, honey." Jack Henry got my attention. "Are you talking to me? Or them?"

"Them." I glared at Jack Henry. He knew that meant to hush up. I turned back to Cephus and Digger. "I'm not going to work on either of your cases tonight. I need a break from both of you. Do you understand me?"

They didn't bother to respond; they both just disappeared.

"I guess I don't need to ask what that was all about." Jack Henry held out his arms and I dropped down into them.

The small kitchen wasn't quite the romantic place I had hoped to be kissing my boyfriend, but if it was all I had, I was going to take it.

Chapter 23

It was one of those nights where Jack Henry had decided to sleep over. The alcohol didn't do the job of relaxing me like it should have, nor did my time spent with Jack Henry.

My mind turned over and over about the murders and how they had to be all connected plus the arson.

Jack Henry did tell me that he finally got his squad car and found Granny at the cemetery, sitting between Earl Way and Granddaddy. He said that he had to tell her to come to the station as a formality, but she wasn't being charged with murder and her little escape through the square didn't help matters. It made her look more guilty.

We also talked about the old mill. He said that

the land did indeed belong to Leotta and although he couldn't accuse her of murder since there was no body and no one had suspected Cephus of being dead, he did question her on the arson.

She claimed she hadn't been out there in years. It was something Cephus took care of. The last time she had gone was when some hippies had been camping in the caves and found the place, making it their home.

Jack Henry said that hippies could've been the ones to torch it if they saw me in there. They were good at making bombs and being resourceful. I kept my mouth shut. It sounded like an ignorant statement for him to believe, but he was the cop, not me.

I was also happy to hear that he did talk the Spearses into an autopsy on Digger's body. That would definitely help clear Granny's name and the funeral home, making Charlotte Rae happy. Though the results wouldn't be in for a few days.

In an election, a few days was the whole election. Granny's chances of winning were becoming slim to none. As much as she told me to hide my crazy, she had hers out on display for the world to see.

I sat in the family room so as not to wake up Jack Henry. He was out of it, happily snoring away. I played with the piece of paper I had taken from Fluggie Callahan's office, trying to reason with myself on what I was going to say to these bookies.

I dialed the first one.

"Hello," he answered.

"My friend Cephus Hardy sent me to you." It sounded like a good way to start to see if he knew Cephus.

"Don't know him." The end of the line went dead.

I had heard these bookies were sensitive as to who they worked with. I wondered if Cephus was as lucky as he claimed. Most bookies wanted their clients to lose. Wasn't that how they made their money?

I dialed the next guy and the same thing happened. Slowly, I dialed the last, hoping and praying he was the one. If he wasn't, I was going to have to start over and try to find out more about the gambling ring. Maybe stop by to see Dottie Kramer.

"Yeah, what about him?" The bookie on the other end didn't hang up on me.

"I wanted to make a bet," I whispered into the phone when I heard Jack Henry make a loud snore and become silent. That was generally when he woke himself up. But the snoring started back up. I continued, "He just gave me your number and said to call. I don't have the particulars."

"It's a five-hundred-dollar up-front fee. Five-hundred-dollar minimum bet and right now I've got the high-school basketball teams on the docket." He was matter-of-fact.

Five hundred dollars?

"Our meet-up place is on the line of Sleepy Hollow and the Watering Hole. Put your cash along with your bet in a gallon plastic Baggie. You walk into the Hole, go to the men's bathroom, and stick it in the first men's stall inside the tank at midnight." He paused. "You got that? Midnight. You sound like a girl so it might be difficult to get it in there, but you women are resourceful. Unless you're some sort of high-pitched freak."

"No, I'm a girl. I'll be there at midnight." The clock on my wall said it was already eleven thirty. I had to haul ass if I was going to run through the ATM, grab the cash and get to the Watering Hole before midnight.

I tiptoed around my place, trying to get dressed and gather the plastic Baggie and note. I didn't bother looking at the time because it would have only made me anxious.

I knew I had made pretty good time but didn't

realize how good until I walked into the Watering Hole and looked at the time on my phone. It was ten minutes 'til midnight.

"Here for an ice-cold Stroh's, are ya?" The bartender pulled a can from his secret Stroh's stash and already had the lid popped open and sitting in front of an open stool. I moseyed over but not without taking a look around to see who was the bookie. "You are pulling a late one. Is your boyfriend joining you?"

"No." I eased myself into the saddle. I put the bottle up to my mouth.

"Hot damn!" Cephus scared the shit right out of me and the beer sprayed out of my mouth across the bar, hitting the bartender right in the face.

He grabbed his bar towel and wiped off his face.

"I know that beer isn't old. I just ordered some new for the just in case." He eyed me.

"I'm so sorry." I shook my head and apologized profusely. "I just wasn't prepared for a fresh one."

The bartender wasn't happy and he made his way down the line. The stools were taken, the pool tables were full and the jukebox blared. There were only two empty tables near the stage where the local bands sometimes played but that was it. Who knew the Watering Hole was still hopping this late?

"I know you said not to bother you, but I know the smell of an ice-cold Stroh's, even from the Great Beyond." Cephus was in panic mode. He stood across the bar where the bartender was with an eager face.

Slowly, I blew a steady stream of air in front of me. Cephus sucked in all he could, smiling the whole time.

If there was a way I could get him a Stroh's, I would, but this was going to have to do.

"You want another one?" the bartender asked. I nodded my head yes and pointed to the bathroom. That way he would put the fresh one on the bar to save my seat while I made the drop-off.

There was no way I was going to leave my cash in a toilet bowl for just anyone to take. I was going to see who went in and out of that bathroom and get some answers about the big payoff for Cephus.

I came to the conclusion that men were nasty. How could they not aim into that big round pee bowl? And why was the stall dirty?

I grabbed some toilet paper off the roll and used it to lift up the tank lid. I pulled the Baggie of cash out of the waistband of my jeans and slipped it in the tank, replacing the lid and flushing the toilet paper. Thankfully, no one came in the restroom. I slipped back out and went to my fresh beer.

The time ticked away and not a soul went to the bathroom.

"Honey, it's 1:00 A.M." The bartender put my tab in front of him. "Closing time."

"But I'm not ready." I shook my beer to show him there was some left but kept my eye on the bathroom door.

The joint had been cleared. All but me and Cephus Hardy plus the bartender.

I wondered if the bookie had seen me and tried to wait it out until I left.

"Listen, I'm going to clean the bathrooms. You can finish your beer, then you have to go," he warned, and grabbed a bucket full of cleaning stuff.

"Damn." Disappointment settled in my gut. I glanced over at Cephus. "I was hoping to meet your bookie tonight. He said you won a bunch of money and I wanted to see if he was the one who could've killed you."

"Nah, he's harmless." Cephus shook his head.

The bartender came back after a few minutes. He put the bucket back and turned around.

"You're going to have to leave now." He smiled and nodded toward the door.

Reluctantly, I threw my legs over the saddle and started for the door after I stuck the only few dollars to my name on the bill. Then it occurred to me. If the bookie used the Watering Hole, I bet I could ask the bartender. He seemed to know everyone in here.

"Say," I turned back around. "Do you happen to know the bookie that Cephus used? He uses your first stall as his drop-off."

Slowly, the bartender turned around. He grinned. My wad of cash in his hands.

"I dee-clare, you're Hoss." There wasn't anything that would've shocked me more. "Why didn't you say something the other night about being a bookie?"

"I told you Cephus had a big payday." He slid the money across the bar back to me. "And I knew it was you on the phone. So when you just sat here, I figured you were waiting to see who the bookie was."

I eased my butt back on the saddle, sideways, and was still stunned.

"I ordered more Stroh's after you came in here because I could tell you weren't finished with me." Hoss nodded. "Am I to expect that cop boyfriend of yours too?"

"Nooooo." I wanted to make it clear that Jack Henry was in no way, shape or form supposed to know I was here. "He would kill me if he knew I was snooping around."

"Well, you seemed a lot more legit than that reporter that sticks her nose where it doesn't belong." He took a glass off the clean stack and pulled the tap of beer, filling it to the top. He took a nice long guzzle. "Ah." He licked the foam from his upper lip. "After a long day, I allow myself one beer. So what do you know about my buddy?"

"I know that he's been missing for quite some time and his family is worried." Now that I knew who the bookie was, I was sure he didn't have any involvement. "Tell me how this works and how Cephus got involved."

"Cephus spent a lot of time in here. Just like anything else, he got to know the regulars, then became one." Between sips of his beer, Hoss used the towel slung over his shoulder to wipe down here and there. "You hear things. Cephus was good at hearing stuff that he shouldn't have gotten involved in. He started out with the ponies, race cars, then got into the school sports. University of Kentucky versus Louisville, those types of bets."

"And you just kept letting him stay here and spend his hard-earned winnings instead of take it back to his family?" I knew it was a low blow, but it was true.

Even though Hoss seemed like a fairly nice guy, he was still a con artist.

"I tried to cut him off a few times but he wouldn't hear of it." Hoss moved on to cleaning more glasses. "The last bet was his last bet. I told him that."

"You mean the last bet he'd ever place before he?" I made the knife sign across my neck. "Um . . . disappeared?"

He looked like I had two heads asking such a thing. "The last bet I was ever going to place for him."

"What was it?" I was curious.

"He knew what he was doing." He shook his head. "He wanted to place a bet on the state wrestling championship."

"Wait." I pulled back. My mind exploded with the past few days and all I had learned about Cephus and his family. "He was betting on his son?"

I recalled the pictures in the newspaper of the state finals and how he lost.

"Wait. You said it was his biggest payday yet." I gulped. I couldn't believe the words were about to leave my mouth. Hoss just stared at me. "You mean to tell me, Cephus bet against his own son?"

Slowly, Hoss raised his head, then lowered it.

"Do you happen to know who he wrestled against?" I asked as the fear knotted around my throat, almost choking me.

I probably didn't need to see what Hoss had to show me because I had already figured it out in my head. Only my heart wished it weren't true.

Hoss pulled out a sack. "It's all there. Ten thousand dollars. Plus the article."

I had never seen ten thousand dollars. I unrolled the top of the bag and peeked in. There it was. All that cash. On top was an article from the Lexington newspaper. I pulled it out.

There was a photo of the winner with a big smile on his face. The headline read, DIGGER SPEARS WINS STATE CHAMPIONSHIP UPSETTING PREDICTED WINNER.

"Oh my God. Teddy." I looked up at Hoss. "Hoss, please trust me with this money. I promise to give it to Cephus's widow, Leotta."

"Sure, but why do you think he bet against his own kid?"

"I don't know, but I think his kid found out about it and killed him." I grabbed the bag and put the article in it before I rushed out the door.

"Emma Lee, don't you dare," Cephus warned me. He ran beside me as I darted out of the Watering Hole and into the parking lot. "Don't you dare."

"Don't you listen to him." Digger Spears appeared. "Yes, you better. I bet you are right, that the sore loser couldn't take it that I beat him."

"Shut up or I'll take you out right here, right now." The two of them danced around the hearse.

"Emma Lee, I'm begging you. I don't care to stay here in the Between as long as my boy, my precious baby boy." Cephus broke down into a full-out cry. Sobbing.

Digger and I stood there watching him. It was heartbreaking to see a grown man cry. Especially one who had just found out that it was his own son who had murdered him.

"I'm sorry, Cephus. I can't let him get away with two murders." I knew in my heart Teddy had also killed Digger Spears. "Digger, your daddy said you hadn't been back since high school. Was that the last time you saw Teddy?"

He looked up in the air, scratched his head, and said, "You know, you're right. I haven't been back and before I left, Teddy told me that if he ever caught me back in Sleepy Hollow, he was going to wring my neck for beating him and embarrassing him like that."

The more he talked, the more it made sense that Teddy tried to kill me that day at the old mill. How did he know what I was up to?

My phone chirped a text. I grabbed it out of my back pocket and looked to see who it was. If Jack

Henry woke up and found me gone, I was going to have some explaining to do.

Cephus and Digger both looked over my shoulder. My hand shook and I immediately got sick to my stomach, right there in the parking lot of the Watering Hole. It wasn't because I'd had too many ice-cold beers. It was the picture of Granny tied up to her moped and the words that read *Meet me at the mill. Come alone or she goes up in flames just like the mill did.*

It wasn't signed and I didn't recognize the number, but I knew who it was from.

Teddy.

Chapter 24

"Oh God, Emma Lee, what are you going to do?" Cephus was so upset he could barely ask his questions.

"I don't know, Cephus." I zoomed back to town as fast as the hearse could go and made it to the other side of town in record time. "I guess I'm going to have to see what he has to say."

"I never thought he was capable of this." Cephus didn't look up. He kept his head down.

"I'm sorry, but I think he needs to be taught a lesson." Digger was fuming.

It was time to tune out the ghosts and try to figure out what I needed to do. Granny was by far the most important person in my life and I would do anything to save her.

The old mill was only a shell of what it was a few days ago. The charred smell filled the air when I got out of the hearse. There were still smoldering coals and puffs of black smoke from the ashes.

"Hello? I'm here." I called out into the dark midnight air.

"Are you alone?" Teddy called back.

"Yes. I would never do anything to hurt my Granny. Though you would," I murmured.

"Follow the blinks." Teddy clicked a flashlight off and on a couple times.

I did what he said and walked over. He lit a kerosene lamp once I was there and I could see that Granny was fine. A little pissed. But fine.

"Let her go. She's an old lady," I encouraged him.

"I would, but I'm not sure I can." Teddy stepped into the light. He had a sawed-off shotgun pointed at me.

Cephus and Digger Spears appeared next to Teddy. Digger was doing some sort of wrestling move while Cephus cried and begged Teddy to put the gun down.

"I love you, son. I forgive you," Cephus tried to reason with him even though he knew Teddy couldn't see or hear him.

"Why, Teddy?" If I was going to join Cephus and Teddy on the other side, I was going to do it with all my questions answered.

I eased my hand in my back pocket and pressed the record button on my phone in hopes someone would find my body and find a phone with a confession on it.

"Why what, funeral girl?" Teddy teased. "Why did I kill my dad?"

"Your dad loved you." I wondered if I could appeal to his sensitive side.

"My dad didn't love me. He didn't love my mom or my sister. I accepted that." His words were filled with hate. "My dad drank away all the money we had. Then he bet on my match. The biggest match of my life and he bet against me."

"How do you know that?" I questioned. I knew it, but how did he figure it out?

"He bet our house mortgage on it," Teddy spat. His bald head shone in the moonlight. "I overheard him on the phone with his bookie saying he was betting the house against me. All the equity in the house. There wasn't much."

"Yeah, you wimp!" Digger swayed back and forth with his arms out like he was about to attack Teddy.

"I couldn't do that to my mom. She was going to

be left out in the cold. I didn't give a shit about his sorry ass. So I threw the match so he would win that damn bet." Tears streamed down his face. His hand with the gun dropped to his side. "I knew my mom had become friends with Vernon Baxter, so even before the match, I told my dad I saw Vernon and Momma make out. It was a lie to get my dad over there."

Cephus stood there, taking it all in.

"I waited in the bushes to see what was going to happen. I wanted Vernon Baxter to beat the shit out of him. When they didn't come to blows, I called Vernon's house so he would go inside, leaving my dad outside." He jerked the gun back up and pointed it at me. "When my dad wasn't looking, I jumped him. Put him in a Teddy Bear Sleeper Hold, but I didn't stop there. It killed him. I took off his ring and flung it into Vernon's garden so the idiot police would find it. I dragged his body into the woods because I knew they would find him eventually."

"Were you nervous for days?" I wanted to keep him talking.

"Hell, yeah. When nobody found the ring or his body, I just went on with the tale that he left on his own. It was rough on Momma, but I didn't care. It was better than the life she had with him." He sucked in a big deep breath. "I was good until I came back here and saw that idiot Digger Spears. He made fun of me. I told him I was going to kill him if he ever came back to Sleepy Hollow and I kept my promise."

"How did you know I was looking into it?" I asked.

"You mean this?" He pointed to the old-mill skeleton. "Easy. Mary Anna started asking questions because she said you were asking about Dad. Terk Rhinehammer was also looking into it and I needed to stop you both. You know the day you went to the courthouse and asked all those questions from the clerk when we were standing outside campaigning with Bea Allen?" he asked.

I nodded.

"I gave the deputy clerk a signed headshot of my new WWE promotional photo and asked her what the funeral girl wanted. Since it's all public knowledge, she was all too generous with her information. I knew the old mill was where the Sleepy Hollow paper was produced and that my dad put the smackdown on that bitch who ran it because she was going to expose him for gambling. Not to mention that the old mayor, Anna Grace May, was in on the gambling. She's the one who didn't let any store owners rent to the bitch paper lady."

All of my questions were being answered.

"It was a bonus that she"—he pointed the gun at Granny, who closed her eyes as Teddy continued—"was fighting with Digger. After I snuck up on him and hit him, he fell in and drowned." He told me the exact same story that Digger had told me and how Digger came to his own death. "I had to get you somehow. I grabbed one of those obnoxious signs and drove it right through his dead heart."

Cephus sat next to Granny. His head was buried in his hands. He sobbed. Digger continued dancing around in circles like he was waiting to make his move.

"Now I'm going to have to get rid of you and her because that dumb-ass boyfriend of yours couldn't solve a crime if it was laid out in front of him."

I watched in slow motion as Teddy brought his arm up and focused the gun on Granny. Shots rang out and like a cannonball I shot across the grass toward him.

He fell, hitting his head so hard against the ground it shook underneath me.

"Stay back, Emma Lee," Jack Henry called out into the nighttime sky just as lights from several police cars turned on, illuminating the darkness.

Cephus stood next to his son's lifeless body, begging Digger for forgiveness.

"See ya, Emma Lee," Digger Spears called from the tree line. "I'm counting on that beer when you cross over."

I smiled. One day I would make good on that beer, but not anytime soon.

"Are you okay?" Jack Henry didn't bother checking on me. He was next to Granny, untying her from her beloved moped.

"A little shaken, but I'll be fine." She stood up and dusted herself off. "I've got an election to get back on track. If you'll excuse me."

"Oh no you don't." Jack Henry took her keys. "You need to come down to the station along with Emma Lee to give a statement."

Jack Henry pushed Granny's moped; Granny was spitting mad. She cursed and said that she didn't have time to worry about convicts and killers. Jack Henry didn't pay her any attention. He hoisted the moped in the trunk of his cruiser and tied it down.

"You go with Emma Lee," he instructed Granny, and came over to give me a big kiss.

"How did you know where I was?" I asked, knowing that I had left him sound asleep.

He let out a big snore and pulled the piece of

paper with the editor's names on it. "You know I'm a light sleeper. How on earth did you think I didn't hear you rummaging around trying to find clothes?" He grabbed me up and kissed me on the head. "I followed you to the Watering Hole and sat in my car until you came out. Then I followed you here. After I saw the flashlight flicking, I knew something strange was going down. I also knew you weren't going to call me, so I called in backup."

"My hero." I batted my eyes the way Granny had taught me.

She always told me to never underestimate a good eye bat.

Chapter 25

It took Leotta almost a week for her to accept the fact and the confession that Teddy had killed his father and Digger Spears. She also had a hard time taking the money I had told her was Cephus's savings.

I couldn't bring myself to tell her that he had bet their life savings, their equity in their home, on his last bet. Jack Henry went along with me about finding the money in a box at the mill. Mary Anna was a different story. She was glad that the fate of her father—though not the outcome they wanted—had finally been figured out.

Right before Teddy was taken to the state penitentiary, he came to and he told Jack Henry where he had buried Cephus's body. In a box in the woods near the old mill. Jack Henry hired John

Howard Lloyd to go out there and dig until they found the box.

There was nothing left but some bone dust and the clothes Cephus Hardy was wearing the day he went to confront Vernon Baxter. Short-sleeved plaid shirt, polyester taupe pants, brown belt and white, patent-leather shoes.

Mary Anna had cleaned the clothes for her momma. They wanted to bury Cephus in those clothes.

The election results were too close to call the night of the election. The town council stayed up all night and hand counted all the votes. Granny lost by two votes and she already had it in her head who the two were.

Though mad, Granny did take some carrot-cake muffins over to Burns Funeral Home as a peace offering. I went with her to make sure she didn't get into any scuffle.

"Is the new mayor here?" Granny swallowed her pride and asked Bea Allen, who answered the residence door of the funeral home.

"He's gone to the office already." Bea Allen's voice accelerated. "What's that?" Her eyes were drawn to the plate Granny held.

"I wanted to bring over a little congratulations offering." Granny lifted the edge of the tea towel she had placed over it. "Carrot-cake muffins. I knew O'Dell likes them."

"That was mighty nice of you," Bea Allen said.

Bea Allen grabbed the edge of the plate. She tugged harder. Granny was having a hard time letting go. I put my hand on Granny's arm to encourage her to let go.

"Did you get the carrots from Dottie Kramer?" Bea Allen asked, and lifted the tea towel to take one more look.

"Hell no." Granny stomped. "She voted for O'Dell even though I told her I would make sure Sanford's goats wouldn't get out again."

I nudged Granny. The lie needed to end. Granny sabotaged Sanford and Dottie.

"Granny has her own special recipe and that is it." I smiled. "Did you ask O'Dell about the newspaper proposal?"

Over the past few days, I had had coffee with Bea Allen. I still had to make good on my promise to Fluggie Callahan. Bea Allen thought it was a great idea to bring back a small-town paper. If anyone could talk O'Dell into anything, it was her.

"O'Dell said he would consider it," she noted.

"Okay, we better get going." I took a step backward. "Today is Cephus Hardy's funeral and we need to get back."

"I do have to say that *we* here at Burns were saddened when Leotta didn't lay Cephus to rest with us." Her emphasis was on we.

"We?" I couldn't just let that one slip by like I did most of her emphasized words.

"Yes." She pushed up the edges of her frizzy hair. "I have enjoyed my time back in Sleepy Hollow working with O'Dell on the campaign. I thought I would take over the funeral home while he runs the town."

"I've heard enough." Granny grabbed my arm and squeezed it. "Congratulations. Let's go."

I wanted to stay and argue the fact that she had never gone to school to be an undertaker, but she would give me some line that she was going to manage the place. It was a lost cause. My dreams of O'Dell's closing Burns Funeral or taking fewer clients because the job of mayor was going to take up his time was just a flash in the pan.

"The feud continues," I muttered, as Granny and I made our way back to the hearse.

I wanted to give myself a swift kick in the butt.

"That's my girl," Granny said proudly.

We both rode in silence as I drove back to Eternal Slumber. We pulled up and John Howard Lloyd had already taken down the big billboard of Granny that took up all of the front lawn of the funeral home. Charlotte Rae was probably pleased as a peach to have it down.

There was already a line out the door and down the sidewalk for Cephus's funeral.

We walked to the back of the funeral home and made our way into the viewing room. Charlotte Rae gave a slight nod when she saw me. Granny made her way over to the gossip section. People were still asking her about coming eye-to-eye with the shotgun. Every time she told the story, she added something that never happened. Soon the story would be that Granny did some sort of ninja move, taking down Teddy.

"Doesn't he look good?" Leotta hugged me around the waist when I walked up.

Leotta had insisted on an open casket even though there was no body. Mary Anna had placed Cephus's clean clothes in the casket. She had blown up a large photo of his face and tucked it inside the collar of the shirt. His gold ring with the large, square, black onyx lay on his chest.

"Yes. He looks great." I rubbed my hand down her arm.

I stood by the casket for a few minutes. Cephus was still there. He hadn't really bothered me a lot over the past week, but he wanted to spend time with his family before it was time for him to cross over.

Cephus meandered over to the group from the Watering Hole seated in the front of the viewing room. He laughed out loud a couple of times as they told Cephus Hardy stories.

"We are so sorry for your loss. We always enjoyed him." Hoss tucked an empty Stroh's can next to the empty outfit in the casket.

The creaky chair in the front caught my attention. I had to make a note to oil it. A funeral was like a coming-out party or just as important as a wedding in the South. There was no need for a squeaky chair.

Granny nearly fell out of a chair in the row behind the squeaky chair, straining to see O'Dell Burns walking through the crowd. Everyone extended a hand of congratulations. Graciously, he nodded and made sure not to take away from the funeral.

I excused myself from Leotta and made my way through the crowd.

"I want to ask a favor from the mayor," I said, and took him to the side.

"Sure, Emma Lee." He rubbed his hands together. "What can I do for you?"

It was the opening I needed to help complete Cephus's journey to the other side.

Chapter 26

My heart warmed as we made our way through town as the citizens who didn't know about or come to the burial pulled their cars to the side of the road out of respect for Cephus.

No matter how much I complained about the small town, the politics and the gossip, it was times in need that made me most proud to live here. No matter what your differences, everyone pulled together to become a strong community.

I did a couple of laps around the square in the hearse before I pulled into the cemetery. The hearse wormed its way around the curvy roads. Trees lined the road, creating a nice shady canopy over the procession to Cephus's final resting place.

John Howard Lloyd sat on the digger; the claw covered in fresh earth.

"Guess that's where I'm goin'." Sadness dripped out of Cephus's mouth.

He looked out the hearse's back window. The car behind us was the family car, in which Leotta and Mary Anna were being driven by Charlotte Rae.

"I guess Vernon Baxter can take care of my Leotta." Cephus pointed to me. "But when she comes to join me on the other side, she's all mine. Forever."

"Forever," I confirmed, and put the hearse in PARK.

This was the second hardest part about being a Betweener. The first was accepting I had a new client who had been murdered. The second was saying good-bye.

I waited in the hearse while John Howard did his thing. He opened the back of the hearse door, had the pallbearers line up and hit the button to start the automatic wheels to set the coffin in motion for them to pick up.

Everyone gathered under the tent and took a seat in one of the fold-up chairs. The pallbearers placed the coffin on the display table in front of the tent.

O'Dell Burns showed up right on time to make good on my favor. Cephus watched as he continued to kneel beside Leotta. It was heartwarming how he tried to console her. Mary Anna snuggled Leotta as they both cried.

I took the brown bag from O'Dell and peeked inside. I handed the bag back to him.

"Mayor Burns has been so gracious to overlook our 'dry county' law this one hour we have together to say our good-byes to Cephus Hardy." As I spoke, O'Dell handed out cans of ice-cold Stroh's to the mourners. "I'd like to send Cephus off with a good ice-cold Stroh's." I deliberately left off the "h." I held my can in the air. "Cheers!"

"Cheers!" the crowd erupted.

The sound of the cans opening sounded like little pops of firecrackers.

"Thank you, Emma Lee." Cephus went around the crowd, taking big sniffs from everyone with a can.

He took one long last whiff from Leotta before he was gone.

Ding, ding, ding.

No one else seemed to hear the ringing of a bell. Maybe it was Cephus telling me he made it to the other side, like the quote in the movie *It's a Wonderful Life*.

Ding, ding, ding.

The second set of bells ringing got my attention. I glanced over the crowd and into the old section of the cemetery.

Ding, ding, ding.

There was a bell on an old stone that was blowing in the wind. Only for me, the dings were too deliberate to be the wind.

The bell was attached to a string that hung down the stone.

While everyone said their final good-byes to Cephus, I walked over to the old stone and noticed that the taut string ran into the ground.

I stepped back and looked at the stone. The chiseled words read *I told you I was sick. Mamie Sue Preston,* scrolled in fancy lettering.

Ding, ding, ding.

I looked at the bell. An older, short woman, with a short gray bob that was neatly combed under a small pillbox hat and wearing a pale green skirt suit, was doing her best to sit ladylike on the stone, with one leg crossed over the other. Her fingernail tapped the bell, causing it to ding.

I couldn't help but notice the large diamond on her finger and the strand of pearls around her neck and on her wrist. And with a gravestone like that . . . I knew she came from money.

"Honey child, you can see me, can't you?" She grinned, not a tooth in her head, but a cane in her hand. "Can you believe they buried me without my teeth?"

I closed my eyes. Squeezed them tight. Opened them back up.

"Ta-da. Still here." She tap-danced over her own grave.

"Don't do that. It's bad luck," I repeated another Southern phrase I had heard all my life.

"Honey, my luck couldn't get any worse than it already is." Her face was drawn. Her green eyes set. Her jaw tensed. "Digger Spears just sent me, and I passed Cephus Hardy on the way. He told me exactly where I could find you."

She leaned up against the stone.

"Let me introduce myself." She adjusted the pill-box hat on her head. "I'm the wealthiest woman in town, Mamie Sue Preston, and I can pay you whatever you'd like to get me to the other side. But first, can you find my teeth?"

I tried to swallow the lump in my throat. This couldn't be happening. Couldn't I have just a few days off between my Betweener clients?

Read on for a sneak peek at the next Ghostly Southern Mystery!

A
GHOSTLY MURDER

Available October 2015 from Witness!

Find out where it all began!

A
GHOSTLY UNDERTAKING

and

A
GHOSTLY GRAVE

are available now!

D*ing, ding, ding.*

The ornamental bell on an old cemetery headstone rang out. No one was touching it. No wind or breeze.

The string attached to the top of the bell hung down the stone, disappearing into the ground. To the naked eye it would seem as though the bell dinged from natural causes, like wind, but my eye zeroed in on the string as it slowly moved up and down. Deliberately.

I stepped back and looked at the stone. The chiseled words *I told you I was sick. Mamie Sue Preston,* were scrolled in fancy lettering. Her date of death was a few years before I had taken over as undertaker at Eternal Slumber Funeral Home.

Granted, it was a family business I had taken over from my parents and my granny. Some family business.

Ding, ding, ding.

I looked at the bell. An older, petite woman, with a short gray bob neatly combed under a small pillbox hat and wearing a pale green skirt suit, was doing her best to sit ladylike on the stone, with one leg crossed over the other. Her fingernail tapped the bell, causing it to ding.

I couldn't help but notice the large diamond on her finger, the strand of pearls around her neck and some more wrapped on her wrist. And with a gravestone like that . . . I knew she came from money.

"Honey child, you can see me, can't you?" she asked. Her lips smacked together. She grinned, not a tooth in her head. There was a cane in her hand. She tapped the stone with it. "Can you believe they buried me without my teeth?"

I closed my eyes. Squeezed them tight. Opened them back up.

"Ta-da. Still here." She put the cane on the ground and tap-danced around it on her own grave.

"Don't do that. It's bad luck," I repeated another Southern phrase I had heard all my life.

She did another little giddyup.

"I'm serious," I said in a flat, inflectionless voice. "Never dance or walk over someone's grave. It's bad luck."

"Honey, my luck couldn't get any worse than it already is." Her face was drawn. Her onyx eyes set. Her jaw tensed. "Thank Gawd you are here. There is no way I can cross over without my teeth." She smacked her lips. "Oh, by the way, Digger Spears just sent me, and I passed Cephus Hardy on the way. He told me exactly where I could find you."

She leaned up against the stone.

"Let me introduce myself." She stuck the cane in the crook of her elbow and adjusted the pillbox hat on her head. "I'm the wealthiest woman in Sleepy Hollow, Mamie Sue Preston, and I can pay you whatever you'd like to get me to the other side. But first, can you find my teeth?"

I tried to swallow the lump in my throat. This couldn't be happening. Couldn't I have just a few days off between my In Betweener clients?

I knew exactly what she meant when she said I needed to help her cross over and it wasn't because she was missing her dentures.

"Whatdaya say?" Mamie Sue pulled some cash out of her suit pocket.

She licked her finger and peeled each bill back one at a time.

"Emma Lee." Granny waved a handkerchief in the air and bolted across the cemetery toward me.

Her flaming red hair darted about like a cardinal as she weaved in and out of the gravestones.

"See," I muttered under my breath, making sure my lips didn't move. "Granny knows not to step on a grave."

"That's about the only thing Zula Fae Raines Payne knows," Mamie said.

My head whipped around. Mamie's words got my attention. Amusement lurked in her dark eyes.

"Everyone is wondering what you are doing clear over here when you are overseeing Cephus Hardy's funeral way over there." Granny took a swig of the can of Stroh's she was holding.

Though our small town of Sleepy Hollow, Kentucky, was in a dry county—which meant liquor sales were against the law—I had gotten special permission to have a beer toast at Cephus Hardy's funeral.

I glanced back at the final resting place, where everyone from Cephus's funeral was still sitting under the burial awning sipping on the beer.

"I was just looking at this old stone," I lied.

Mamie Sue's lips pursed suspiciously when she looked at Granny. Next thing I knew, Mamie Sue was sitting on her stone, legs crossed, tapping the bell.

Ding, ding, ding. "We have a goner who needs help!" Mamie Sue continued to ding the bell. "A goner who is as dead as yesterday." She twirled her cane around her finger.

I did my best to ignore her. If Granny knew I was able to see the ghosts of dead people—not just any dead people, murdered dead people—she'd have me committed for what Doc Clyde called the Funeral Trauma.

A few months and a couple ghosts ago, I was knocked out cold from a big plastic Santa that Artie, from Artie's Meat and Deli, had stuck on the roof of his shop during the winter months. It just so happened I was walking on the sidewalk when the sun melted the snow away, sending the big fella off the roof right on top of me. I woke up in the hospital and saw that my visitor was one of my clients—one of my *dead* clients. I thought I was a goner just like him because my Eternal Slumber clients weren't alive, they were dead, and here was one standing next to me.

When the harsh realization came to me that I

wasn't dead and I was able to see dead people, I told Doc Clyde about it. He gave me some little pills and diagnosed me with the Funeral Trauma, aka a case of the crazies.

He was nice enough to say he thought I had been around dead bodies too long since I had grown up in the funeral home with Granny and my parents.

My parents took early retirement and moved to Florida, while my Granny also retired, leaving me and my sister, Charlotte Rae, in charge.

"Well?" Granny tapped her toe and crossed her arms. "Are you coming back to finish the funeral or not?" She gave me the stink-eye along with a once-over before she slung back the can and finished off the beer. "Are you feeling all right?"

"I'm feeling great, Zula Fae Raines Payne." Mamie Sue leaned her cane up against her stone. She jumped down and clasped her hands in front of her. She stretched them over her head. She jostled her head side to side. "Much better now that I can move about, thanks to Emma Lee."

Ahem, I cleared my throat.

"Yes." I smiled and passed Granny on the way back over to Cephus Hardy's funeral. "I'm on my way."

"Wait!" Mamie Sue called out. "I was murdered! Aren't you going to help me? Everyone said that you were the one to help me!"

Everyone? I groaned and glanced back.

Mamie Sue Preston planted her hands on her small hips. Her eyes narrowed. Her bubbly personality had dimmed. She'd been dead a long time. She wasn't going anywhere anytime soon and neither was I.

Get cozy with

CAROLYN HART's
award-winning
DEATH ON DEMAND mysteries

dead by midnight

978-0-06-191498-0

A recent death appeared to be suicide, but
mystery bookstore owner Annie Darling suspects murder.

laughed 'til he died

978-0-06-145308-3

Mystery bookstore owner Annie Darling and her husband, Max,
plunge into a startling web of danger when a trio of deaths
is linked to their island's youth recreation center.

dare to die

978-0-06-145305-2

Annie and Max Darling are caught in the middle of
a devastating storm of rage, secrets, and murder
when they invite the sad and beautiful Iris Tilford
to their party at the pavilion.

death walked in

978-0-06-072414-6

A mysterious woman caller leaves word that she's
hidden something in the antebellum house Annie and Max
are restoring. When Annie finds out, she hurries to the
woman's house, only to discover she's been murdered.

CHD1 1211